I0586986

AMONG US

KRISTINA RIENZI

INDIGO HAWK
GROUP

AMONG US

Copyright © 2018 Kristina Rienzi

This is a work of fiction. Names, characters, places, and incidents either are the product of the author's imagination or are used fictitiously, and any resemblance of fictional characters to actual persons living or dead, business establishments, events, or locales is entirely coincidental.

All rights reserved. No part of this book may be used or reproduced in any manner without written permission from the author and publisher except in the case of brief quotations embodied in critical articles or reviews.

Paperback ISBN: 978-0-9969721-6-1

Book Layout: Kate Tilton (www.katetilton.com)

Cover Design: The Killion Group Inc. (www.thekilliongroupinc.com)

Editor: John Adamus, The Writer Next Door (www.writernextdoor.com)

Proofreader: Christie Stratos, Proof Positive (www.proofpositivepro.com)

Author Photograph: Jaime Lynn Photography (www.JaimeLynnPhotography.com)

Indigo Hawk Group
Shrewsbury, New Jersey

For Kate Tilton, my author assistant extraordinaire! Your encouragement, expertise, and unwavering support push me to greater heights. Thank you for believing in me as an author—and a person.

CHAPTER ONE

1968

SIX-FOUR WITH A BUZZ cut and two stars on his shoulder, Major General Lou Rollins hopped into the mud-covered all-terrain vehicle. Strapped with every weapon and tool a military man on an alien hunt might need, he revved the crappy government engine. The easterly wind lifted pinpricks of rain droplets left behind from last night's rainstorm. They found their home on Lou's face. No waiting for them to evaporate. Passivity was for civilians. He shook the spit-like water off and hocked a loogie to send a message.

Never mess with an armed man on a badass, far-out mission.

Lieutenant General Dowd's leathery face flashed before Lou's mind's eye. He grunted. An invisible scar where Army-career-suicide had pressed the barrel of an M14 to his temple niggled at him. His credibility was about to bleed out on the side of Highway 35. It was worth every AB+ pint.

Lou unrolled the coffee-stained map from the passenger's seat. He pulled it taut until the wrinkles disappeared.

Sliding the tactical flashlight from his belt, he turned the illumination on. The thin paper appeared translucent against the darkness. He traced his finger along the route from where he was to where he needed to be. His sense of direction was stellar. Lou was a human compass, reading the stars to find his way at night. The map verified his hunch. Due west. He crumbled the sheet and tossed it on the floor. No stinking wood fibers would make a bit of difference. It was time to trust his gut. And the universe.

He pressed the gas and plodded along the uneven land. If evidence of those bastards existed, he would be the one to find it. He didn't give a rat's ass if it was those little gray men. Shit. He would take anything inhuman with or without a heartbeat, whether they had hearts or not. He meant anything. The green kind. The reptile kind. The insect kind. The kind he hadn't yet imagined. Not because he was crazy. Because they existed. Any quantum physicist worth his Ph.D. would agree. Tonight was Lou's one shot to prove to those pompous assholes whose butt cheeks were sewn together that they didn't corner the market on intelligent life in the universe. Not a chance in holy hell.

White-knuckling the steering handles, Lou slammed his size twelve boot on the gas pedal. His two front tires barely jumped before landing back on the marshy ground with a splash. Mission popping-a-wheelie-for-kicks had failed. The damn UFO had crashed in the worst possible spot—three miles from the ocean, knee deep in the wetlands after an east coast deluge bordering on a tsunami.

His pulse quickened. Sure as shit, a futuristic, disc-shaped invader belonging on the other side of the universe could be taking a nap in his backyard. The urge to yell *yee haw* nearly took over. He threw his shoulders back instead.

No mountain man here. Strictly highbrow Army all the way. Although his deviant shadow-self disagreed.

Lou strategically maneuvered the military vehicle through the thick molasses of terrain at sloth speed. He was getting nowhere fast. Soggy soil devoured what was left of the tread on his oversized tires. He rose and sank along with the ATV as if he was driving over a wet sponge. The topography betrayed him big time. He punched the dash. Speed. Force. Anything was better than trudging through the sloshy territory. He hit the pedal to the floor, pushing the ATV to its breaking point. Instead of gaining ground, the driver's side tire hit a log buried below the quicksand-like dirt. For a split second, the vehicle skidded into a fishtail. The back tires swung out scarcely enough behind Lou to half dump him into the mess below.

He hung onto the side of the truck like a monkey in a tree. Heaving his torso back up to the wheel, the massive bicep he had grown in the weight room came in handy. He struck the side of the road pig with his boot as clumps of earth propelled into the darkness. Back upright and focused, the nervous rush had him seeing stars. Lou blinked a few times until his vision cleared. A puffed-out chest later, he regained control of the hunk of metal and rubber. Squelching over the landscape, he closed in on his bull's-eye inch by inch. When he had gone about one hundred feet, he slowed to a stop.

Gangs of crickets cried aloud in a cacophony of distant chirps. Squirrels scampered frantically through the trees. They weren't running away from the quad. Adrenaline rushed Lou's veins. Closer than he had ever been to a possible otherworldly object, he lifted the night vision binoculars to his eyes. The moonlight glinted off a spark of silver shrouded by oversized trunks and branches. Was it a plane or a spaceship? He couldn't tell. Only a sliver of the crash site was visible through the dense wood. No wings protruded. No tail lifted from the darkness. No lights. No sounds. No gases, flames, or screams. He caught a glimpse of the only observable section from his vantage point. A curve like a bubble, possibly a disc, was like nothing he had ever seen on a plane—be it private, commercial, military, or otherwise.

Lou's mouth went dry. He swallowed to create natural saliva. His tongue was like a dehydrated prune. What was he thinking, refusing to take a partner on this mission? He had no idea what he was up against. Damn cocky ego refused company. He wanted all the credit, Army suicide or not. If he were the smart armed forces leader he had been trained to be, he would have acquiesced. Maybe Dowd had the answer already. Lou was simply his chump.

He shrugged off his discontent, inhaled the moist air, and jerked the side-by-side around a group of trees. Turning left toward the moonbeam's only reflective target, for the first time in his life, he hoped he didn't see what he wanted to see most.

As Lou got closer to confronting the object face to face, his stomach clenched. If someone, or something, were inside the craft and alive, he would really drop a load in his pants this time. Ego was his bitch. To suspect aliens exist was one thing. To find proof was another. To experience their existence would be life-changing.

The radio beeped. Lou silenced it. The last thing he needed was an unexpected signal, or an unannounced voice coming through the speaker to declare his arrival on the path of extraterrestrial danger. The faster he debunked the weather balloon, the better off he would be.

His final trek to the mysterious object was a blur. When

he arrived, he shut off the engine. Thick woods wrapped him in an eerie blanket of silent darkness. Soundlessness defied all logic. Fear of the unknown hung in the air like a curtain. Lou wouldn't speak. Whatever was out there might hear him.

He fell back in his seat. No longer standing, he drew in a breath as if it were his last. It might be.

Lou narrowed and widened his eyes in rapid succession. His vision alone couldn't be trusted. Awe and fear swirled inside his gut like marble rye. An honest-to-God illusion stared back at him. Mouth agape in wonder; he reached for his radio without breaking his stare on the thing that couldn't exist.

But did.

CHAPTER TWO

PRESENT DAY

MARCI DIPPED the long lighter into the smoky glass vase on her gothic-style dresser. She pushed the trigger a few times until the fire grabbed the wick of her sage—for a reason—candle. Flick. Light. Burn. The pillar shone unsteadily in the oval mirror, creating an eerie halo. Jagged flames rose and fell, finding their sweet spot before the haunting luminescence settled in for the night. Supernatural ambiances made her house feel like a home.

She exhaled. Pure Zen. All her negative energy evaporated into the amber glow. Dr. Simon, the strait-laced professor, nosedived into the fire until she disappeared. Rebel-with-a-cause Marci emerged like a rocket from the smoke.

Die, day bitch. Die.

The mirror's image was of a skinny—*no, thin*—girl she liked but hardly recognized. A glimpse of her 3-D black butterfly tattoo peeked out from under the strap of the loose-fitting camisole. Wings inked with a fluttering effect seemed to lift off her skin. A butterfly ready to take off in flight. Like the one inside of Marci. Pain. Death. Change.

Where was Marci in all the chaos? Numb. Caterpillar to butterfly stage or not.

Marci pressed her hand on the new flat of her stomach and sucked in her gut. Finally. She was a size small again. Thirty-pounds still haunted her. They were dead and buried. They couldn't come back. They weren't welcome. She would slice them up like a sushi chef if necessary. Committing murder wasn't beyond her.

She smiled at her new likeness. She loved her new self. Those pre-bedtime rituals were precisely what she needed to boost her ego. A necessity to endure her mundane life. Unfortunately, another day would come, like all workdays, when she was forced to adopt her alternate persona.

The one that was a lie.

Marci strutted, shoulders back, her hips left to right as she sashayed down the non-existent runway leading to her queen-sized bed. She hopped onto the too-thick mattress and slipped under the navy satin sheets. The horror anthology she was dying to read winked at her from her neoclassical nightstand. A Himalayan salt lamp gave off the perfect gleam of light to smoothly transition from her form of story-based meditation and right into dreamland. Truth be told, the honey pepper whiskey helped, too. Even better yet—it sang her favorite nightly lullaby.

Drink me...

A blue hawk, Jersey Shore University's logo, stared at her with judgmental eyes. She gave the bird the bird. Caramel-colored liquor swirled inside the mug. Shards of ice clinked together in the clay made for coffee or tea. Not booze. She took a long, delicious gulp, cursing the jerks that gave it to her. Welcome-to-the-university-gift her ass. Brown-nosing was more like it.

A numbing burn matching her soul slid down her

throat. It warmed her from the inside out. Her shoulders couldn't hold on to the tension any longer. They finally gave way to relaxation. Alcohol fought more demons than any overpriced therapist.

When the nasty bird landed on its coaster, she dove into an evil fantasy. Dark fiction embraced Marci. Her reality was a betrayal. Her pretentious so-called literary genius colleagues would never approve of her bookish decisions. Or her choice of nighttime remedies. Thankfully, the bright whiskey-drinking, horror-loving professor didn't give two shits. Everyone had secrets. And a dark side.

Two paragraphs in, a rush of unease filled the room. Marci paused. She searched for an unseen presence hiding in the darkness. Shadows appeared. They belonged there. Candlelight swayed on the dresser in a subtle warning.

Danger is coming for you. There's nowhere to hide.

Marci slammed the anthology shut. Goosebumps grew on her arms like a fungus. Her thermometer was set at a moderate seventy-some-odd degrees. She still shivered. A foreboding lurked in the darkness.

She tossed the book on the half of the bed reserved for a man who didn't exist. A distant rumble of thunder echoed. Marci flinched. The sound transformed into deep drumming. It escalated, creeping closer and closer. For a moment, it quieted. Then it roared with intensity outside her bedroom window.

Marci's neck muscles stiffened. Tightness spread to her shoulders like lightning. It shot down her spine, arching her back. Fight or flight mode: activated.

She launched upright. The covers flew off her body. Twisting to the right, she swung her legs until her toes dangled above her skull slippers. Putting them on one by one, Marci pushed off the mattress to investigate.

Before she got her footing, an unnerving boom bellowed. The center hall colonial vibrated as if a mega-Taser zapped it. Marci clutched her nightstand. The second-floor collapse was imminent. She tightened her grip. Thousands of pounds of heavy furniture were about to hurtle through the floorboards. Marci braced herself. Broken bones weren't an issue. Her expensive stainless steel appliances being crushed to bits were another story.

She cringed. Nothing happened. The roar. The shaking. Everything gradually slowed to a stop. Dead silence.

Marci's nervous system raged on fire. She was jittery. Unsteady all around. She chugged the last of her self-medication to calm the popping in her core. Her orthodox academic reputation was overdue to headbang with a hangover. Whiskey breath was Marci's truth.

With an empty bird, she anchored her foothold and headed toward the window. Three steps away, everything went full dark. Her candle's flame, the lone light remaining, waved a fiery finger at her. *I told you so.*

Something was out there.

With her thumb and forefinger, she separated the two-inch slats on her faux gray wooden blinds. She peered outside. Nothing stood out. Except for the darkened street lamps, the cul-de-sac was status quo for a typical suburban school night. Doors remained shut. Cedar Lane was empty. Nothing stirred.

The magnitude of the all-encompassing darkness, which had camouflaged the blacked-out SUV parked in front of her neighbor's house.

Power outages were commonplace at the Jersey Shore on blazingly hot summer days. Not at nighttime. Not nearly autumn. A transformer could have blown nearby. The lack of moonlight was inexplicable. If the light from the moon had gone out, Marci need not worry about a noisy bump in the night. The world was screwed.

Marci gazed up into the night sky. It was gone. No stars. No moon. No clouds.

Her lips began to tremble out of control. She couldn't turn away. She was fixated on the strange object suspended above.

Dark childhood memories deluged her like thirty-foot rogue waves. Marci sunk below the surface of the ocean in her lungs. She couldn't breathe. Stumbling away from the all too familiar sight in quick, jerky steps, she tripped over her own feet. Steadying herself, she doubled back from the window as if escape was possible. Her hamstrings hit the mattress. She tumbled onto to her bed.

Emotionally drowning, images swirled around the whirlpool in her mind. Marci pressed her hands to her head. She wanted out of her time warp. Back to reality. Now. The impressions were too vivid. Too clear. Too real. They would never let her go.

Strong mental currents dragged her under the tide. She plummeted deep into the images she had locked away forever. Graphic, terrifying recollections played on a loop in her mind.

Marci remembered everything. It wasn't pretty.

CHAPTER THREE

KEEPING deadly secrets was Pierce's zero-guilt pleasure. Lying to his new wife was a tad more complicated.

Intense nutty aroma of the one hundred percent private reserve Kona coffee wafted throughout the mini-mansion. It unearthed memories of Oahu where his honeymoon still lingered. Pierce chased the scent into his six-figure custom kitchen. He would never get his money back. He didn't care. Pocket change like that was easy to come by when you had no moral boundaries.

Mrs. Austin spun around. Wavy hair cascaded in a blond waterfall over her fragile frame. Her oversized smiled sparkled first thing in the morning. Ten years his junior, he saw babies every time he looked into her eyes. He often looked away.

Lindsay handed Pierce a large Ravens mug filled to the brim. He took a long sip of the Hawaiian beans brewed to perfection. Pierce kissed her on the forehead. He slipped onto a bar stool at the granite island. His stomach growled and churned. Pierce was hungrier than he thought. Life on the road meant eating a lot of fast food. A home cooked meal would be heaven.

"There's no place like home."

Lindsay raised her eyebrow. "You could've fooled me."

"Work is life. A necessary evil." An evil he loved.

"I thought I was your life." Lindsay opened the refrigerator door.

Her *poor me* was loud and clear. "What are you making?"

"Scrambled eggs and bacon."

"Toast?"

"Yep."

"Something happen at school?" Pierce's heart raced. If she quit, she would be all the way up his ass. He didn't need that in his life. Not now. Not ever.

"Nope." Lindsay balanced a tub of butter, the egg carton, a package of bacon, and a half-gallon of milk between her thin arms. She dropped their breakfast-to-be on the granite countertop and plugged in the toaster.

His ass was his own. "Need help?"

Lindsay shook her head. She opened the cabinet above her head and pulled a small bowl down from a shelf. Quietly, she cracked six eggs into the bowl. After adding a splash of milk with a sprinkle of salt and pepper, she whipped the egg mixture with a fork.

Pierce lifted his gaze from the latest electric racecar he was admiring. A morning in peace was all he wanted.

"What's up?"

Lindsay shrugged. She lit the burner under the frying pan and turned it to low. After shoving the whole wheat bread into the toaster, she poured the mixture it into the pan. Runny eggs sizzled.

He forced a sincere-looking grin. "Spill it."

She sighed. "I hate living alone."

Round two.

"Last time I checked, I live here."

"On paper."

"We drink coffee together. That's an old married folk requirement. We've already moved up the spousal ladder."

"We should be together more than we're apart."

He clenched his jaw. "We'll escape again. Soon. Just like Hawaii. Only better."

"Right."

Pierce swallowed his annoyance. "How's Bora Bora sound?"

The moment the words flew out of his mouth, he winced. What was wrong with him? Wooing her at every turn wasn't the answer. He was creating an entitled monster. Their life was their life. Love. Lies. Loneliness.

His wife leaned into the hand on her tilted hip. She wasn't buying his discounted sales pitch this time.

"I don't need Bora Bora. I need a weekend at a Virginia winery. I want to live like every other normal couple."

Pierce let the remainder of his frustration evaporate and met his wife at the counter.

"We *are* a normal couple. My job may be inconvenient, but it's hardly stopping us from having the life we want. I take business trips a few times a month. Big deal."

"A few too many."

Pierce made a gesture to touch her waist. "I'll make it up to you this weekend. I promise."

Lindsay slithered away from him. She layered bacon in between paper towels on a plate and put it in the microwave. He wrapped his arms around her from behind and pressed up against her.

"We can start now."

An aroma of sizzling meat and eggs on the skillet filled the air. The spatula scraped against the bottom of the frying pan as Lindsay pushed the eggs around.

"I love you, Mrs. A.," he whispered in her ear.

The toaster popped. Lindsay pulled the toast out and put it on his plate. Pierce turned her around slowly. He locked onto her tearful expression. It pulled at his heart.

"This six-thousand-square-foot home. Your special order cherry-red Jaguar."

"Uh-huh."

She blinked away the droplets forming. Pierce ran his hands down her arm, landing on her ring finger, which he wiggled back and forth.

"Three-and-a-half karats. What other auditors make my kind of money?"

"Don't know."

"None."

The microwave beeped. Lindsay popped the door open, pulling out the shrunken bacon.

"You're worth all of it. Every minute I'm away from you, I miss you. I sacrifice everything for you to have a better life. Don't you see that?"

Lindsay shut off the gas burner. She kissed Pierce with passion. He pushed her up against the countertop, and his temperature rose. His heart began beating wildly. Her heart was pounding, too. He could feel the thumps through her silk nightgown. Right before they took their understanding of each other to the next level on the granite, the house phone rang. They both shuddered. Pierce kept kissing his wife as he side-eyed the phone. The only calls he would get on that line were either from his parents, who were cruising to Bermuda, or work. He let out his angst and pulled away from his wife.

"I think..."

"Get it."

Lindsay rolled her eyes but married it with a smile. He kissed her on the cheek and then grabbed the phone.

"Pierce Austin."

"Are you sitting?" His partner was on the line.

"Hardly. Who's bombing us now?"

Miles only called for a global emergency. "NASA."

Pierce pulled the phone away from his ear. "I need to take this call. Can you bring the food upstairs?"

"Go."

Lindsay waved him away. Pierce grabbed his coffee and jogged up the hardwood stairs. Once in his office, he closed the door.

"Talk to me."

He took a hearty sip of his bold coffee, preparing him for what Miles would say. If NASA was involved, it was terrible news.

"Some hotshot is looking for a promotion. Maybe he has a suicide wish. Either way, his story just made our jobs a hell of a lot harder."

"That story's bullshit."

Pierce logged into his laptop. He clicked the Internet link feverishly. His search engine was jamming up.

"Everything's bullshit. Until it's not." Sarcasm shaded Miles's tone.

Pierce came upon an article of a man in New Jersey who reported seeing a UFO over the beach. He didn't even click on the link. That level of nonsense wasn't worth wasting data on.

"We turn the story into bullshit," Pierce said. "That's what we're trained to do."

"Not when there's evidence. Ridiculously huge evidence." Miles's voice was lined with fear and anger.

The spinning rainbow wheel of online torture flew around Pierce's screen. He pressed the *return* key seven times. Not like overdoing it was going to help. He felt better, which was a plus.

"Damn Wi-Fi."

"Don't bother. Documented UFO sighting over the Jersey Shore."

Pierce guffawed. "Amateur-level garbage. What else?"

"Beach bum dude wasn't the only person who spotted the craft. A pro videographer dabbling in astronomy captured some convincing footage."

Pierce typed away furiously to restart his old piece-of-shit government computer. He needed an upgrade. Yesterday.

"So what? He altered the tape. That's the story we'll tell. Fake footage."

Miles sighed. "Tell that to the slimy bastard in the video."

Pierce stiffened. News of a worse kind wasn't possible. Revelations of that nature ended careers. And lives. He rolled his chair away from the computer.

"The ESA will never let NASA get away with this shit."

"Too late. The tape has already been released to the media. That NASA media whore is married to some big shot at Channel 7."

Pierce paced frantically. "Don't tell me you're worried about this bullshit? We'll make the story disappear like it never happened. The loser with the evidence will be no more. Poof. Gone. Done."

"Our hands are tied, my friend. NASA's rep is either being framed or we're losing the war."

The words coming out of Miles's mouth, the man nick-named *The Terminator* at the government's most secret deadly agency, were terrifying.

"God. No." Pierce rubbed his forehead.

"God? There is no God. God wouldn't make aliens. Let alone put them on Earth. Whatever made those ETs is pure evil."

"You have your beliefs."

"What we believe means nothing. What the masses believe will take us all down. We've got some damage control to do."

His office door creaked open. Lindsay dropped the plate of bacon and eggs on a tray table and left the room.

When the door clicked shut, he asked, "What do you need from me?"

Miles cleared his throat. "How fast can you pack a suitcase?"

Pierce threw his head back. After what he had just told Lindsay, he felt like an asshole. He pawed his hand through his hair. Work before life. Or death.

"Consider me packed."

"Add a windbreaker. You're on your way to the infa-mous Jersey Shore."

The media had given that part of the Garden State a gaudy and obnoxious reputation.

"The Jersey Shore? I'm tempted to tell you to count me out."

"No can do. Your assignment is an English Professor. She moonlights as a blogger."

"Did I miss my demotion letter?"

"She lives on Cedar Lane. Her neighbor is Retired Army General Rollins." Miles paused. "1968 Lou Rollins."

Pierce's heart flew out of his chest. He looked at his watch.

"No time to chat. I've got a bag to pack."

"That's the secret agent I remember. Once you're settled, I'll send more information."

"Roger that." Pierce hung up the phone.

"How's breakfast?" Lindsay texted.

Pierce glanced at the article that finally came to life on his screen. He texted his beautiful but naïve wife back. "Simply delicious."

CHAPTER FOUR

MARCI POUNDED on her neighbor's wooden front door three times in rapid succession. *Boom. Boom. Boom.* She cringed at the resounding echo. Her conservative professor get-up didn't fit the guise of an obnoxious neighbor. Out of her daytime character? Totally. Warranted? Hell yeah.

Slowly turning to inspect Cedar Lane, the street was all clear. No angry retirees in bathrobes waving morning papers in the air. Everybody's front doors were shut. Perfect picture of stillness.

Lou wasn't responding either. He was the only person she could talk to about what happened last night. The only one who would validate her. Understand her. He had to answer the door. Soon.

From afar, his living room blinds appeared to be closed. Marci hopped onto his lawn to investigate. Her kitten heels sunk into the mossy grass. She pulled them out to try to gain her footing on top of the ground. They dropped back in again. Useless. Dew sprinkled her jet-black knee-highs, plastering them to her feet. Marci took careful baby steps to prevent the disheveled outfit look that was frowned upon at her haughty university. Scarves and stockings were their runway look.

Three medium-sized rose bushes lined the outside of his bay window. Marci maneuvered through the angry shrubbery, careful to avoid a thorn attack. She met the oversized pane face to the glass. Examining the window up close, it was clear. The slats were tilted downward and not touching. The angle created a slight gap and a favorable semi-panoramic first-floor view. Outlining her face with cupped hands, she pressed her nose against his window to spy.

His living room was dark. An empty rocks glass sat alone on the coffee table. His crocheted blanket was rolled like a cigar on the worn leather chair.

She reclined backward to glance at the small kitchen window on the other side of the house. The one above his memorial garden. The one she had no intention of destroying. Marci leaned onto the glass instead. She twisted sideways to get a glimpse of his kitchen from the inside. No lights were on.

Lou never slept this late. Marci's heart jumped Double Dutch. Her thoughts ricocheted like they were in a pinball machine. Dead. Taken. Vanished. She pulled her phone out of her blazer pocket. After unlocking the screen, she stared at her wallpaper photo of the Milky Way. For a beat, her tense muscles relaxed. She tapped the 9, then the 1.

Lou wasn't dead. Taken. Or vanished. He was sleeping late. She needed to get a grip. Marci tapped the *end* icon. She paced his uneven pavers in short, tight circles until she dizzied. Way to work out her latent anxiety. Replace it with nausea.

Her watch's alarm buzzed. She jumped. Fifteen minutes left until she had to get on the road for work. It was the final countdown.

Answer the door, Lou.

Marci stretched her tightened neck, the birth of a headache looming. Glancing at her phone again, she considered calling to wake him. Time was running out. She needed to see his face. Talk to him. Tell him everything.

She doubled back a few feet onto the walkway and eyeballed the second floor. A light flickered in the room above the kitchen. Lou's bedroom was in the same location as in her house. Every colonial on Cedar Lane was identical. Shadows crossed in front of his window for an instant. Lightness filled her chest, then released.

Back at it. Marci pressed his doorbell five times in a row. She paused. No answer. She pushed it five more times then knocked on the door like his house was on fire. Too bad if the neighbors burst out of their homes screaming. Let them throw rocks at her. She would call the cops herself. Waiting too long was over. She bounced on her toes for a few more seconds. With her finger readied to push the doorbell another five times, the retired Army General's door cracked open an inch.

Only the hook and chain separated Marci from her grumpy—but alive—neighbor. Lou's shock of perfectly shaved military-style white hair greeted her before his annoyed grunt.

"Who croaked?" he asked with a pinched expression. "Better be somebody good."

"Thank God. We need to talk."

"Good morning to you, too." He closed the door in her face. The lock clanged. The door unlatched.

Marci pushed past Lou into the foyer of his circa 1970 center hall colonial. "Morning."

"Coffee's on." He guided her into the kitchen with his buff yet wrinkled physique.

"You have a to-go cup for me?"

"Nobody kicked the bucket, did they?" Lou pointed to the pantry.

"Maybe. But nobody we know."

He put his extra large soup-bowl-turned-mug on the counter. "What's got your goat so early?"

Marci pulled the wooden bifold pantry doors open. They creaked. She scanned the stocked pantry and then grabbed a paper cup and plastic lid from the third shelf.

"You'll never guess what happened last night."

"I had insomnia again." Lou cleared his throat in an *eh-hem*.

Marci turned on her heels. It took a second for his words to sink in. "You saw?"

He gently took the cup from her. "Big deal."

"Big deal? It's proof. Now we can..."

"It won't change anything."

Marci met him at the counter. "Telling the world will."

He poured the hot coffee into the small cup with care. "You know the drill."

Marci pulled the stainless steel refrigerator door open. She searched amongst stacks of plastic containers filled with left-overs for the hazelnut-flavored creamer. Lou reserved them for her impromptu visits. The creamer hid behind the nonfat milk. She maneuvered the bottle out and dropped it on the counter.

"We're not the only ones."

Marci pulled up the picture she took a screenshot of last night after panic mode had retreated. She turned her phone toward Lou. The article titled "They're here" showed a photo of a man in cargo shorts and a plaid button-down shirt pointing to the sky stared back at them. He was on the promenade near the beach a few miles away.

He shrugged. "The media will say the article is fake news."

"I read the article."

"I bet the story reads like fake news."

"That guy saw the same UFO that flashed across the sky at thousands of miles an hour before the craft disappeared. We don't have the technology to build something like that."

"You'd be surprised. Military advancements would blow your mind."

Marci scrolled to the next picture on her phone. It was the man's sketch of the craft. The UFO was flat and disc-shaped with a ring of triangle lights around the perimeter. He reported the beams of laser-looking lights cycled through the colors of the rainbow, projecting a stunning Ombre display in the sky. She pointed the photo in Lou's direction.

"I've seen a UFO like that one before."

"You think?"

"In 1998."

"Oh boy."

"There's something you're not telling me."

"They're getting bolder."

"They?"

"For another time."

"We have to do something. Tell someone."

"Tell who?"

"Report the sighting to the police. NASA. The Army. You tell me, General."

"It's best if we say nothing." Lou handed Marci the coffee and a spoon.

"Wrong answer."

"Our power outage explains everything. A transformer blew."

Marci poured the creamer into the coffee cup. She mixed her drink together with vigor, splashing some on the counter in her haste.

"That's a lie."

"Lies are subjective." Lou wiped up her mess.

Marci snapped the plastic lid on top of the paper cup. She took a long sip. Hot and delicious. Lou was the best barista in town.

"I'm not supposed to say anything, knowing what I know?" She put the spoon in his sink.

Lou shot Marci a curious glance. "What do you know exactly?" He took the creamer from her and put it back in the refrigerator.

"A blacked-out SUV parked on our street. Whoever was in that truck watched the UFO hover over all of us. When the UFO disappeared, the truck took off like it was at the starting lineup of the Daytona 500."

Lou raised his eyebrows. "NASCAR? I had you as a golf fan."

"Michelson all the way. Sprinkled with a little Ricky Bobby. And my love of moonshine."

"From your days in West Virginia?" Lou chuckled.

"Don't change the subject, old man." She smiled sternly.

"Fair enough."

"I need to tell everyone about the UFO. I won't sleep at night if I hold this story in."

"Don't sleep. Write your novel. Alien-government conspiracy stories make for bestselling fiction and block-buster movies. Sell your script. Quit that energy-sucking vampire of a day job you hate."

"That vampire pays the bills." Marci straightened. "I'm serious. I can't keep that kind of secret to myself."

Lou leaned up against the counter. "Let me get this straight. Instead of playing it safe, you'd rather broadcast to the world that the government stood idly by as an alien spaceship hovered over your cul-de-sac in the middle of the night?"

Marci bit her lip. "That's what happened."

Lou wrinkled his forehead. "Or did it happen? Maybe you were dreaming. Or hallucinating. Better yet, maybe you didn't have your glasses on."

"I don't wear glasses. We saw an alien spacecraft."

CHAPTER FIVE

"IT DOESN'T MATTER if that is what we saw last night or if we had x-ray vision and psychic abilities. If you talk about this insanity to anyone, God forbid the cops, you'll be suffocating in a strait jacket before you can blink."

"You're overreacting." Marci's tone was sharp.

Lou took a sip of his black-like-his-attitude coffee. He menacingly raised his eyebrows.

"Stress can trigger a psychotic break. Or the Army can induce a mental health issue. Take your pick."

Marci fastened the top button on her jacket. "Fine. I'll just publish my post on *Among Us* then. The draft is ready to go."

"Bad idea."

"If there's backlash, I'll say it was an experiment—an excerpt from my novel-in-progress."

"The one that doesn't exist?" Lou pinched his lips together.

"Notes exist."

"You're up against the same risks. Try to pass *Among Us* off as fiction, and you'll be discredited as a serious writer.

Blogs are meant to be non-fiction. You'll be deceiving your readers. They'll lose trust in you. Is that the reputation you want?"

"Fair enough." Marci's voice hardened. "I need to stand by my truth. It's all I have."

"Say nothing."

Marci rolled her eyes. "Have we met?"

"Trust me on this one."

"If a general doesn't support the First Amendment, we're all doomed."

Lou leaned in the doorway between the kitchen and the foyer, crossing his legs.

"You know as well as I do there's no such thing as freedom of speech. We're all doomed no matter what you say. Or don't say. Haven't you figured that out yet?"

"I need to do something."

Marci slowed to a stop before she reached the front door. Her gaze fell to the white ceramic tile below. Lou lifted her chin.

"You're one person. It's not your job to save the world, kiddo."

She believed it was. "One person who wants to try."

Marci headed for the door. Enough was enough. He wouldn't change her mind. It was made up. And then some. Every cell in her body told her to publish her post on *Among Us*. How could she not? Her followers deserved to know about her experience. It was proof to them, if for no one else. Lou had no clue about social media. Transparency was everything.

A prickle of tension loomed in the back of her head. Marci paused mid-step. She rolled her next to try to release the stiffness. Lou's oversized, callused hand gently gripped her bicep. She spun around to face him.

"I'm running late."

"You're willing to trade your life for a story no one will believe?"

"It's an under-followed blog. Not the nightly news."

"You never know. Anyone could be reading your work. Even the president."

"Yeah, right."

"You're already out there. Website. Blog. Anyone can find you."

"No one's looking."

"Not yet."

Her head began to tighten. "They're only words."

"Coming from an English professor? You know better. Words have tremendous power."

"I'm harmless."

"Our government doesn't discriminate when it comes to top secret information."

"I'm not worried."

"Do me a favor."

"No promises."

"Don't publish the blog post. Don't tell anyone about the UFO last night until you research everything you can on this topic. Don't take any chances. The military taught me one thing: never challenge the government. They'll retaliate with an endless vengeance. You'll never recover."

"It's a blog post, Lou."

Lou's gaze darted as if in memory. "If you manage to survive."

Marci's head began to pulsate. She forcefully relaxed her rigid posture.

"I promise I'll be okay."

"You can't make that promise." Lou's pursed lips quivered.

"I can. I have."

Lou stared at her in a serious-as-cancer manner.

"Controversial allegations about the government's awareness of alien visitation could cost you everything."

"I'll be admitted to the psych ward before the government ever considers me a threat of any kind."

"It doesn't matter. It is true. It happened. They know it. You know it. They'll know you know it."

"You're overthinking everything." Marci's head pounded alongside her conscience.

"No. You're not listening to me." Lou's face reddened with each drawn out word.

Marci sighed. "Go ahead."

"They know about the visitation. They likely had a hand in their arrival. And more. Exactly as you're suggesting. They're privy to all information. Including your under-followed blog. Internet activity. Text messages. Everything and anything you assume is private. The last thing they want is for you to go public with what happened. You saw what you saw. Keep your mouth shut if you want to stay safe."

Marci narrowed her eyes. "Not going to happen."

"You can't go telling stories about government conspiracies without cold hard evidence and an army of experts backing your every word. You'll still be scrutinized and discredited. At least you'll have the best possible chance to be taken seriously. Even if only by a handful of people."

Marci made it halfway out the door. She turned around.

"I guess I'll need to get the proper evidence. One way or another. Proof exists. And the good people of this world deserve the truth."

Lou's head dipped. "I believed that once. Before I learned that what people really want is to feel safe."

"Safety is *never* guaranteed."

"Perception of safety keeps people in check."

Marci cleared her throat. "You mean under control?"

Lou took a swig from the oversized coffee mug. A faded Army logo had seen too many years.

"Is it so terrible to feel safe?"

"It is when it's a lie."

"It's not time to talk, Marci."

"I think it is."

"If you ring that bell..."

"They'll hear the chime in DC, I'm sure."

"Big brother and the rest of his family are always watching."

"I'll be sure to wave hello."

Lou spoke in a low tone. "They'll stop at nothing—not even murder—to keep their secrets."

"Thanks for the joe."

Marci raised her hand in goodbye. Without a word, Lou backed into his house and shut his front door. Her watch said she would be late...again. She jogged across the street and hopped into the driver's seat of her truck. With the door closed, the contained silence screamed. Her pounding head was palpable. Throbbing filled the cabin of her car in volume and tension. The boulder of Lou's words had burrowed inside of her mind. They were building a permanent home. She needed a sledgehammer. Better yet, a bulldozer.

Thump. Thump. Thump.

She massaged the back of her neck to find some relief. An old water bottle sat in her center console cup holder. Not BPA free, but it didn't matter. She popped the cap off and chugged the warm and disgusting water. Fishing in her purse on the passenger's seat, she found a travel package of ibuprofen. She finished the bottle with the two pills and prayed the painkiller would kick in soon.

After rubbing her temples, she checked her makeup in the rearview mirror. Lou's house judged her. Clueless civilian. What did she know? Lou had inside information. She was either too ignorant or too headstrong to listen. The colonial's window-eyes watched her every move. Those blinds, blinking their eyelashes in the sunlight at her. *Silly girl. You know not what you're about to do. Maybe if we intimidate you long enough, you'll change your mind. You'll let it all go.*

Marci pulled her eyes away from the homestead's critical gaze. She couldn't escape her mind where the real condemnation lived. Lou or no Lou, her confidence had waned the closer she got to the time to reveal her truth. Something deep inside irked her. She couldn't put her finger on it. The gremlin needed to be silenced.

Before she analyzed what could go wrong and changed her mind, just like Lou and his house wanted her to, she opened the Internet on her phone. Clicking on the bookmark for her town's website, she scrolled past the crime stories and scanned the page. On the middle right side, she landed on a blurb reporting a blown transformer right around the time Marci's house vibrated last night.

Touché, Lou. Touché.

Why hadn't she shown all the evidence to Lou? The picture wasn't nearly enough. In her defense, she assumed he would be supportive of her decision to act. After all their late-night conversations, staring at the stars above, wondering about life on other planets...she never imagined he would deter her. Copping out when the going got tough? Not the general. Never.

Marci clicked on the link to the article she had saved. Her phone connected to the webpage. She gasped. Everything was gone. She stared at the screen in disbelief. Her pounding head returned with a temper.

Thump. Thump. Thump.

Her concentration waned. She wrestled it back. Marci swallowed her fears for the last time. She took a deep breath and logged onto her *Among Us* blog from her smartphone. After clicking on the draft blog post, she read it one last time for good measure.

Now or never. Marci shoved the key into the ignition. The engine roared. So did her adrenaline.

She exhaled and pressed *Publish*.

CHAPTER SIX

THE HEAVIER-THAN-NECESSARY BROWN leather messenger bag pulled Marci's shoulder down. Her small frame slanted to the right. One strong wind and she would tip over. Even weighed down with too much junk, she was breezy and light. Her smile couldn't be contained. The quintessential luggage was a stark yet understandable contrast to the tiny black purse holding the essentials—sheer pink lip gloss, matching wallet, phone, and two keys on a plain ring—hooked on her elbow. She readjusted the bag to lay diagonal across her navy blazer and light blue button-down Oxford shirt. Better to give her already doomed posture a break.

Practically skipping from the extra excitement of the day before, she headed into the crowded hallway. The smell of fresh new semester lingered in the air: old books and new dreams. Students coated the campus like bees in a hive. Marci buzzed along with them.

The English department's chairperson, Ana Stewart, waved at Marci from the other end of the hall. Even from far away, Ana's serious expression was unmistakable. Marci hurried to meet up with her friend.

"How's it going?"

Ana's typically relaxed posture was rigid. "Can we chat?"

"Everything okay?"

Ana checked her watch. "In my office. Will ten minutes from now work?"

A growl escaped Marci's stomach. She clutched her purse close to hide the sound. An off-diet, perfectly toasted onion bagel with cream cheese needed to get in her belly stat. She usually would ask Ana to push their unplanned get together off, but Ana's energy was unsettling

"Sounds good."

"Great. See you then." Ana disappeared into the crowd of students.

Minutes later, Marci pushed opened the glass door etched with *English Department*. Besides a series of book-shelves and couches, the pseudo-reception area (without a receptionist) was empty and silent. She fell onto the velvety cushion of a navy-blue love seat. Her pulse raced. The two-seater couch should have been named the anxiety seat. Waiting rooms of all kinds were never about love. They were about fear. Marci stared at the clock as if willing Ana to appear.

Time ticked away. Ten minutes came and went. Leaning on the armrest, Marci checked email on her phone. After deleting thirty-three junk messages, she clicked the Internet icon. Jersey Shore University's Wi-Fi was insanely slow. It seemed like minutes before she could type in the address for *Among Us*. Just as she began reading the comments on *Among Us*, a shadow darkened her. Marci sensed a presence nearby. She looked up.

Ana loomed over her. "Ready?"

"Let's go."

Ana strode into her office that looked more like a library first. She swung her designer bag on a giant hook next to her full mahogany desk. The Ivy League degrees framed behind her looked down their noses at Marci. She closed the oversized wooden door behind her with a thump. She slid into the leather chair across from her boss. Dark energy thickened into a wall between them.

"What's up?"

Ana typed feverishly on her keyboard. "Hold on."

Marci began to twist her hands in her lap. "Should I be worried?"

With an icy tone, Ana said, "Only if you have something to hide."

Marci shifted uncomfortably in her seat. "What do you mean?"

Ana failed to lift her head from the monitor, click-clacking away on her keyboard.

"Here we are."

"Did something happen?"

Ana stopped typing. A slight, obviously forced smile crossed her face.

"I like you, Marci. I think you know that. I also respect your work. I needed to start our conversation off by saying that because in this context I feel it's important for me to reiterate what I think of you as a person as well as a professor."

"What context?"

Marci touched the crystal bangle on her left wrist. Ana had given the bracelet to her for her birthday last year. Marci searched for her friend in the room. Only her judgmental boss appeared.

Ana rolled her shoulders back. "Jersey Shore University hired me to do a job with several areas of responsibility. One of them is upholding their stellar reputation in academia. As well as in the public eye."

Marci's heartbeat flew from her chest to her throat. She fidgeted with her bracelet.

"What does any of that have to do with me?"

Ana slowly turned the flat screen monitor around. She pointed the screen toward Marci.

"This."

The purple and black website design was all too familiar. Marci's stomach dropped.

CHAPTER SEVEN

ANA'S DEMEANOR TIGHTENED. "I can't overlook certain missteps. This is one of them."

Displayed prominently—and bravely—across the page was the title: *Among Us*. While no pictures of Marci existed, the author's pseudonym of M. E. Simone wasn't much of a disguise. The butterfly logo was an obvious give-away. Anyone who ever met Marci saw a butterfly on her.

She wanted to deny that the site was hers. Make Ana work to figure it out. There was no use. If she believed in truth, truth should prevail.

"It's my labor of love." Marci half-heartedly shrugged.

"Interesting choice of words for an English professor. Your followers don't seem to exude any love at all."

Scrolling through the online backlash, Ana read each comment bashing Marci's recent post on the UFO sighting.

Next, you'll be saying Bigfoot was in your backyard.

You're as insane as your allegations.

Where's the proof? You expect us to blindly believe you with no evidence?

She should have recoiled at Ana's insulting tone. Marci held her chin up high.

"My followers disagree with me sometimes. They still follow me for a reason."

"What reason is that?"

"To question their beliefs. Explore the unknown. They have intense emotions. I love that about my readers. Even if they aren't the emotions I want."

Ana shook her head. "Please tell me I have you all wrong. The Marci I know would never jeopardize everything she's worked for in academia to create an online persona this foolish and insignificant."

Marci hadn't considered that *Among Us* could jeopardize her career. She forced a proud grin.

"It's writer fun. Nothing more."

"If you want to entertain people, write a novel. That would be good press for the university. A published author never hurt business. At least it would be clear what you're writing is fiction."

"It's not fiction."

"That's the problem. When you parade fake information around as potential fact, discussing your absurd beliefs as reality, you're risking your professional credibility over science fiction."

"How is *Among Us*, not in my name, putting my stellar track record in academia at risk? Other professors have blogs. It's never been an issue before."

Ana narrowed her eyes. "Those other professors obtained formal approval from the university before launching their websites. Their content was directly in line with their nonfiction subject matter expertise in education, as well as the university's vision and mission. No comparison here. You never asked for permission. You hid it from us. You lied."

Marci shot forward. "I did *not* lie."

"Jersey Shore University feels you did."

"Correct me if I'm wrong, but we're still in the United States. It's called freedom of speech."

"Freedom of speech doesn't exist in employment. It's why we make you sign employee handbooks, nondisclosure agreements, and more policies and conditions of employment than laws on record."

"It's not like I write blog posts when I'm at work. *Among Us* isn't connected with the university at all. One thing has nothing to do with the other."

"Not true. Your actions outside of the university affect your reputation here as well as ours. If we allow this to continue, we're liable. The university has much more to lose, including the students who have invested in us, than one professor with a wild imagination."

Marci shook. Rage boiled to the surface. She wanted to jump up from her chair and tell Ana off. She bit her lip hard enough to draw blood. Now wasn't the time to lose it. It would confirm everything Ana had said. A snow bomb cyclone would form in hell before Marci allowed that to happen.

"Who complained?"

She couldn't trust anyone. Marci's phone buzzed. Her mom was calling. She pressed a button to send it to voicemail.

"Not important. The issue here is that it exists. And it belongs to you."

"Fine. Do an investigation. You won't find anything. *Among Us* isn't hurting anyone, let alone the university. If anything, it opens minds. Which is what I thought Jersey

Shore University was all about. It's why I wanted to work as a professor here—just like you."

Ana cringed. "There won't be an investigation."

Marci let go of her tight grip on the bangle. A red mark appeared in its place.

"Good."

"Your posts raised enough uncertainty about your mental health for us to take action without one."

Marci clutched the bracelet. Her nails pressed into her skin.

"You've got to be kidding me."

Ana crossed her arms. Her demeanor tightened in clear opposition.

"Your professional judgment is in question."

Marci twisted the bangle around and around.

"I'm as stable and as professional as you. If I weren't, it would have come up sooner. And you absolutely would have addressed it."

"Proof hasn't surfaced before," Ana said.

"My beliefs are my own. I'm allowed to have them. I'm also allowed to discuss them on social media."

"Nothing's private online. Your public image is Jersey Shore University's business."

"My made-up public image. It wasn't like I ran around the university's halls handing out my business cards. I wrote about my passion for the unknown with people who chose to follow me...to argue with me or not...and where I should have been safe from criticism and embarrassment from my employer."

"The moment someone finds out what you're doing, it becomes the university's issue. *Among Us'* suggestions are damning. From an employee performance standpoint, it's blatantly unacceptable—nearly insubordinate. A social media policy violation at best."

"You can't be serious."

"We won't tolerate a respected professor spewing nonsense online while they're trying to represent our university's traditional brand and standards of the highest caliber. Jersey Shore University cannot afford this kind of negative attention. Our enrollment numbers were down this year. We're a private school that depends solely on tuition payments to fund all our programs. We don't get state or federal assistance. If word gets out about your connection to *Among Us*, it won't only damage our reputation, it will crash our already tight budget."

"That's ridiculous. I don't have that kind of power."

Ana let out a deep breath. "Like I said before, I really do like you. But I simply cannot have this happening under my supervision. I am being held accountable here. I hope you understand."

Marci leaned forward toward her arrogant boss. "What am I supposed to understand?"

Ana tightened her expression. "It's best for everyone involved if you take some time off."

"You're firing me?"

Marci grasped the bracelet. She couldn't believe what Ana said. Never in her wildest dreams did she imagine she would lose her job over *Among Us*. Not that it would have stopped her from writing blog posts about aliens. At least she would have been prepared for being reprimanded at some point.

"It's technically an administrative leave. Consider it a long vacation. When things calm down, so long as it's in the best interest of Jersey Shore University, we'll have you back as a professor."

"I have a mortgage." Her voice trembled. She didn't want to sound desperate, but she was.

The corners of Ana's mouth turned down. "You'll receive a reduced rate of pay while you're out on leave."

"I see." Some pay was better than none. Marci should have been grateful. She wasn't.

"You'll also keep your benefits, but you won't accrue vacation time. No 401(k)."

"How long do I need to be on leave?"

"Through the end of this semester." Ana turned the computer screen back to its original position.

Marci let the bracelet fall to the edge of her wrist.

"I'll plan to return after the holidays."

"It's not automatic. That's when we'll revisit your position and let you know."

Marci gripped her wrist again. "I can't just come back to work?"

"Like I said, we'll review your job in a few months."

She shimmied her hand back and forth until the bangle moved closer to the first knuckle on her thumb.

"I get it. No guarantees."

With some pay, maybe she would survive it financially. She had an emergency savings account. Partial unemployment was also an option. Safety nets were popping up all over her mind. She didn't want to risk losing everything she had worked so hard for all her life.

"For today, you'll need to cancel your classes. We'll take care of your schedule for the rest of the semester. I'll be in touch over Christmas break to tell you about the university's plans for next year."

"Should I look for another job?" Marci turned the bangle in slow, deliberate movements on her hand.

Ana paused. "I'm rooting for you, Marci, but it's not

entirely in my control. *Among Us* is damaging. Depending on where it goes...I can't promise you anything."

Her position as she knew it was gone. Marci made her hand small and shifted the bracelet around her bones.

"Gotcha."

"I'm so glad you understand. You can grab your things today, or make some time to come back tomorrow. I know this is a lot to digest, but I want to make it as painless as possible."

Ana stood up, her palms pressed flatly on the desk, dismissing Marci.

Marci's shoulders curled forward. Whether Ana was spelling it out or not, Marci was getting a severance to carry her through the holidays. After that, she was out of a job. Tears began to build behind her eyes. She held steady. It wasn't the time or the place for weakness. She breathed in her pain.

"I'll stop by tomorrow."

"Perfect. Let me know if you need help."

Marci slid the crystal bangle off her hand. She dropped it on Ana's desk with a clang.

"No thanks."

Marci turned her back on her old friend. Her feet dragged on the tile below as she shuffled out of Ana's office. When Marci reached the stairwell, tears made their way down her cheeks.

CHAPTER EIGHT

MARCI TRUDGED her walk of shame from Ana's office. Her stomach's growl had advanced to a roar. She didn't have it in her to stick around. Kissing the onion bagel with cream cheese she never ordered goodbye, she walked right past the university's cafe.

A sudden blaring sound startled her. Marci jumped, nearly shaking. After catching her breath, she doubled back to the cafe's entrance. Peeking her head in to find out what was so loud and obnoxious in the quiet hallway, she checked out the full quasi-lunchroom.

Tony, the stocky chef, pointed the remote control high in the air from behind the counter. Marci tilted toward the doorway and leaned in. A breaking news flash buzzed on the flat screen hanging on the wall. Grabbing the first chair she found at a two-top table nearby, she dropped her bags on the floor and fell into the seat. Tony hushed the lunch crowd. He shouted over the story in his strong Brooklyn accent.

"Listen up. Something big just happened over here."

Cafe patrons paused mid-conversation—and mid-bite—

to take notice. A few of Marci's students slowed to lift their heads from their smartphones. They glanced around as if searching for another explanation for the instantaneous quiet. On the television, Channel 7 news anchor Shirley McMillan shuffled a stack of papers around. Her expression blanched with each passing moment she filled the screen.

"Our darkest fears have been confirmed, our deepest curiosities quelled. Humans are not the only living beings in the universe."

Marci gasped an octave too loud. She covered her mouth with her hand. Yet her brilliant smile pushed through.

Shirley's green eyes stared into the camera. "The world has been contemplating the existence of extraterrestrial life for centuries. From supposed sightings to abduction cases and more. Finally, evidence from New Jersey changes everything. Life as we know it will never be the same."

Marci's body trembled. She had waited her entire life for this very moment.

"Let's go to NASA's press conference, which is about to begin. We're hoping all of the details will be explained so we can understand what this means to humanity."

Bulbs flashed in rapid succession as a middle-aged man approached the podium, arms swinging. An army of poker-faced officials surrounded the space behind him. A red ribbon on the bottom of the news report identified him as Michael Force, NASA representative. The room quieted as Force bent into the microphone.

"Over the last twenty-four hours, UFO call centers have received a flood of reports originating from the East Coast. Callers reported sightings of an oversized unidentified flying object over the New Jersey shoreline that rapidly vanished. Some of those reports have been published online, causing general questions and concern."

Marci straightened. She listened with intensity.

"Much of the actual evidence has been suppressed from the media so a fast and proper investigation could take place. It all began with a story from a local New Jersey man who was the first person to formally report the UFO sighting. After his article was published online, comments skyrocketed into the tens of thousands. As in standard operating procedure, the case was referred to NASA to investigate. We took it from there."

The same article she had read online about the spacecraft reported at the beach near her home had caught NASA's attention. Marci pushed back from the table slightly. The chair legs scraped against the floor. Her heart pounded out of control. This was not fake news. It was as real as news could be.

Force's stance widened. "One of the pieces of evidence that we'll share following this press conference is undeniable video footage of an extraterrestrial being inside of the spacecraft. We're working around the clock to gather more data. This is what know so far."

Marci took stock of the cafe. Slacked mouths abounded. Stunned silence.

"Questions?" Force asked.

He scanned the room. Reporters shot the NASA representative with inquisitive noise. A lanky man in a navy suit standing along the back wall spit his questions out.

"How do we know this isn't another hoax? You guys have denied the existence of aliens since the beginning of time."

Force nodded. "I've personally confirmed it was, in fact, an extraterrestrial spaceship. Next question?"

A petite, blonde-haired woman in the front row wearing a smart, bright red pants suit dove into the volley.

"Confirming an alien was inside the UFO is quite a stretch. Have you also personally had an interaction with the being, or is this just another ploy to use our tax dollars for NASA's benefit?"

Force straightened his posture. "I assure you, this is not about tax dollars. I can't confirm how I know the being is real. I have verified the footage myself. I can assure you it is authentic."

Reporters went wild. Their questions overlapped in a violent flood. Force tensed. He closed his folder abruptly.

"That's all we have for you now. We won't be taking any more questions. Additional information will be forthcoming. Thank you."

Force stormed out of the room with a gang of protective services on his heels. All the muscles in Marci's body clenched as she took in the information she had just heard. She bottled up her breaths to try to calm down. Throwing her bags into the air like confetti wouldn't bode well for her already tainted reputation.

NASA admitted to the existence of aliens. It was the sweet sound of validation.

Marci wasn't crazy after all.

CHAPTER NINE

MARCI BEAMED. Ana would choke on her Ivy League words.

An image of Lou, her strong-willed neighbor, came into mind. He believed. She wondered about his reaction to the news. NASA was behind it. Indeed, he wouldn't poo-poo her today. Nothing she could say or do would ever be questioned again.

She snapped out of her reverie and re-glued her gaze back to the television. The news report flashed to photographs. A video with the reporter commenting in a dark tone came on the screen.

"There you have it, folks. Finally, it's the truth straight from NASA's mouth. We're thankful to our loyal fans all along the New Jersey coastline, who captured high-definition snapshots and videos of the craft from all angles and shared them with us online. We're about to show you the footage we received hours ago. We're just waiting for the permission to release it. After this broadcast, you'll find the images uploaded on our Channel 7 website."

Was it really happening? Marci stared at her palms as

if they held the answer. Still reeling from her quasi-termination minutes ago, she pinched her skin until it hurt to make sure she hadn't passed out and started dreaming. Confirmation was out in the universe. Denial was impossible.

Looks of shock and awe plastered the faces of the cafe patrons. She wasn't alone in her disbelief of what had just happened. She shook her head. Undoubtedly, it was April Fool's Day in September. Marci's churning gut told her differently. All that had happened in the last few days was real.

The reporter smiled, her serious tone shifting to excitement as she prepared to share the details of arguably the most significant news in history. Ratings would soar straight through the roof for Channel 7 today. Raises and promotions for everybody. Emmy Awards galore.

"Let's go to the most compelling evidence of all. We're about to play the video NASA mentioned in their conference. You'll want to take a very close look here. Brace yourself. The footage may not be suitable for children. Now's the time for them to leave the room if they're also watching. The image is shocking at best. Ron Petro, a Jersey Shore filmmaker, captured the footage you're about to watch. The universe has obsessed him since he was a child, often filming the night skies over the beach in hopes of capturing something that would change his life forever. Ron nailed it with the evidence of a lifetime. Here it is."

Gripping footage from Ron's camera displayed on the screen, scanning the sky over the beach in the way a security camera might. A large object moved into view. The camera angle darted to it, taping as it came closer and closer until it covered most of the night sky. Although it may have otherwise blended in with its background, Ron's high-definition equipment made it stand out as a three-dimensional object.

To hell with the amateur footage. Petro was the next Spielberg. His lighting and clarity were adjusted to perfection. An enormous spacecraft came so close into view that it should have been only a blur in the night. Ron had carefully zoomed in on what looked like a square. A large window with a transparent surface, both reflective and transparent, appeared on the side of the spaceship. For a few seconds after, the video's footage was clear as if it had been spotted in daylight.

A gangly, almost iridescent, gray-skinned being floated beyond the windowpane. Intense moonlight illuminated the sheen of an oily substance on its porous skin. Its bald head turned toward the window as if sensing it was being watched. Black, smooth ovals for eyes. Two pinholes where a human nose would be. A slit for a mouth. The being was the spitting image of a character straight out of a high-budget science fiction movie.

Nothing like Marci encountered as a child.

In a breath, the alien swiftly disappeared behind the window. The viewable porthole to extraterrestrial life transformed into a metallic camouflage matching the rest of the spaceship. Then it was gone, too.

The news flashed back to the reporter.

"Cold, hard evidence. You saw it here first. If that didn't take your breath away, I don't know what would. Unidentified flying objects may have been explained away in the past as military planes, but there was no hiding a UFO the size of a cruise ship over the Jersey Shore. Nor the crystal-clear picture of the extraterrestrial being inside of it. Let's get our viewers' reactions on the west coast."

A plump, gray-haired reporter held a microphone, his

lips pressed together in a slight grimace. A crowd of bulging-eyed pedestrians huddled behind him.

"What began in New Jersey as important news has made its way all over the globe as the shock of the extraterrestrial encounter spread. Here's what they said."

Looks of terror crossed the faces of interviewees as they told stories of their own experiences, sightings, and abductions. Others claimed it was a sign the world was coming to an immediate end. A few expressed genuine excitement over the admission, ready to engage with their new interplanetary allies.

Sheer exhilaration in the small cafe was equally evident. Barks of laughter, increasing voice volumes, and incessant chatter filled the room.

Marci's mouth was as dry as cardboard. She reached for the bottle of lemon-flavored sparkling water in her bag. After twisting the top off with urgency, she chugged it. Marci slammed down the empty bottle like it was a beer. Exhaling, she imagined the possibilities of what the shocking news would bring. A small shout of glee disappeared down her throat.

After a deep breath, Marci sent the email canceling her last class of the day as promised to Ana. She cited an emergency. NASA's breaking news was an emergency in her eyes. So was her administrative leave. Her hands trembled in anticipation of typing her next blog post on *Among Us*. A plethora of ideas raced around in her mind. NASA's report spoke for itself. Maybe it was time to reveal her truth. All those naysayers would undoubtedly change their tune.

Marci scooped up her things from the cafe. She ran full speed to her truck. Her keys jangled in her hands. The key fob escaped her on multiple tries to get a handle on it. Finally, she got a hold of it. She pressed the unlock button.

Ripping the car door open, she jumped into the driver's seat.

Her heart morphed into a frozen block of ice in her chest. It started drumming out of control. Her whole body tingled. Shaking the jittery feeling off wasn't possible. It wasn't anxiety. It was elation. Amazement. Overwhelming astonishment. Uncontrollable excitement.

Spontaneous giddy laughter bubbled up inside of her. It flew out of her mouth. The volume of nervous energy filled the cabin of her truck in a blink. It felt like it could explode into bits at any moment.

Marci's thoughts scattered like confetti all around her. She stared at her dashboard as if it were the first time she had ever been in a car. Concentration escaped her. She couldn't think straight. Reasoning as to what had just happened escaped her. Theories scrambled around in her mind. Fantasy was reality. Fiction was fact. It was all too much for her to process with her emotions on high. No logical explanation existed.

But aliens did.

Vindication. Clarity. Hope.

Lucidity stormed her. Chaos became order. Next steps were outlined before her eyes. The time had come.

Validation. Vindication. Victory.

Peeling out of the parking lot, Marci slammed on the gas pedal. She zoomed too many miles over the speed limit. The public confirmation of extraterrestrial life made her breathless. Nothing would bring her down. Not even breaking the law.

CHAPTER TEN

LOU PRESSED the red button on the remote. The big screen television turned off in a *whoosh*. He exhaled his angst. Breaking news, his ass. UFOs were real. Humans were not alone in the universe. Never had been. They weren't alone on Earth either. He had known that for five decades.

He scratched his head. NASA's immediate acknowledgment in response to a suggested encounter threw him for a double loop. He never expected a blatant public admission. No matter the evidence. Videography had been discounted in the past. Mass media had been quieted. People with supposed incriminating information had vanished. Or died mysteriously. Only one plausible reason existed as to why NASA admitted to the existence of aliens.

Survival.

Sweat slithered down Lou's cheek like an angry rattlesnake. It was only seventy degrees in his colonial; hardly warm enough to cause perspiration. His heart palpitations had nothing to do with the third cup of coffee he had powered through either. Something more sinister chewed at his gut. The world had learned the partial truth. It was his duty to fill in the blanks.

The hundred-year-old grandfather clock against the wall read half past noon. Lou parted the curtains and looked across the street. Marci's car wasn't in the driveway. She usually wouldn't be home until between four or five. The news report told him today would be different.

Lou fought with his rational mind. His thoughts warned him against what he was about to do. None of the possible outcomes were good. The truth must come out. He had always known it would happen one day—aliens taking liberties to be recognized. Humans scrambling for an explanation. It was all a farce. The government had always known the truth. They had been a part of the truth.

He stood purposefully. Silently encouraging himself to take the first step toward freedom. Freedom of information. Freedom from the burden he had carried for so long. He had no other option. Not at his old age. He had to be the general he was meant to be.

A hurricane brewed inside of him. The leader put aside his fears to serve. He was far from brave. Blind courage had gotten him through the hardest times in his life. Not just the Army. The tragic loss of his Irene and Eric. Loneliness.

Not bravery.

Blindness.

Lou had waited for a moment like this all his life. His mind was made up. He made the sign of the cross and then kissed the one around his neck. Said a Hail Mary. Said the Our Father. Asked his angels for protection. Covered all the bases. What he was about to do had no reverse button. No redo. All or nothing.

Now or never.

Lou put one committed foot in front of the other. Determination filled him up the whole way. In only a few steps, the basement door appeared. He put his hand on the doorknob and turned it. It creaked. When the door was behind him, he peered downward. The whole way down. Longer than it had ever been, even only yesterday. Each step was one closer to his personal victory.

The ultimate point of no return.

He descended toward the concrete below the old rickety stairs. Gripping the railing, his sweaty palms slid down with ease. Senior knees didn't do the job they used to for him. At his age, he was lucky he didn't have to have surgery to replace them yet.

When his feet hit the floor, he paused. He drew in a deep breath. For his service and more, he was proud. Today's events were the permission he needed to lift the burden of deceit off his heart. If ever there was a time to reveal the truth, it was now.

He made his way to the safe with a steadfastness in his gait. This was his one opportunity to get ahead of the tragedy before his time had passed and he was merely dust in the wind. Lou might be too old to go up against the government. Marci sure was not. She was bright and articulate. A woman with a passion for astronomy. And candor. Marci had guts, too. Even if she didn't see it for herself. Armed with his evidence, she would be unstoppable. Keeping this power to himself would be a waste.

The combination lock *ticked* to the last digit. Before opening the heavy metal door, Lou turned around to make sure no one was behind him. He scanned the far corner of the basement. No one was tucked away hiding from his view. Waiting. Watching. No one was there. Not that he could see anyway. Didn't mean they weren't listening in. Keeping an eye on his every move. Stalking him like the prey he was.

He hadn't touched that deadly piece of paper since it was locked away many moons ago. The mere memory of its existence caused his tiny arm hairs to rise.

Lou slid his shaking, sweaty hand into the safe. He reached to the back wall on the top shelf. The thick paper between his fingers was unmistakable.

Slowly, he pulled the envelope out.

He held the document for a few moments, trembling. Why was he so petrified to reread it? It wasn't like the contents were new news. The ESA was why. Lou's eyes darted around. Had an agent planted cameras in his house? A recorder? Maybe a booby trap? The last thing he needed was for those ESA bastards to take his salvation away from him. At least not until they were exposed for the traitors to humanity that they were.

Lou carefully drew the delicate document out from the envelope. Beads of sweat streamed down the back of his neck. His pulse quickened. Sharp pains prickled his chest cavity. If he didn't know any better, he would think he was having a heart attack instead of a panic attack. He tried to control his breathing—mouth closed, attentively pulling air into his nose, and then pushing it out. No dice. The intensity of his fear took over. Like in the Army, his only choice was to push through it.

The flimsy document lay folded lengthwise in his shaky hand. He separated the folds until it was fully open. The pain had subsided. His heart beat against his chest like a caged wild bird. Squawking and screaming to be freed. Word by word, Lou poured over the contents of the document for the first time in five decades. His digested cereal began to climb up the rocky mountain wall of his aged esophagus. When he was done reading, his breakfast sat in the back of his throat like a volcano waiting to erupt.

Dizziness encapsulated Lou. Dark memories came rushing back with no mercy.

CHAPTER ELEVEN

1968

THE BLACK PEN made a ringing sound when it hit the cold metal table. Rollins exhaled in relief. He had made the right decision. Honesty was his only policy. That is, if he wanted to sleep at night. Recalling the strangest assignment —no, encounter—he had ever had made him shiver.

Surreal.

The door behind Lou flew open. General William H. Dowd strode into the room. His intense energy entered before his physically fit older body. Lou stood and saluted his superior. Dowd gestured for the major to take a seat. Lou obliged.

Rickety chair legs screeched across the floor as the general pulled the chair away from the table. He swung his body around and landed in the seat in one choreographed motion.

Dowd narrowed his eyes at Rollins. "Your report, Major."

"Yes, sir." Lou slid the paper across the table. He held his breath.

Dowd grasped the report in his left hand. He scanned it

in a relaxed pose as if it were the Sunday paper. His eyes moved left to right. His expression didn't shift.

Lou couldn't decipher his superior's reaction. General Dowd was probably writing him off as incurably insane. The product of too many science fiction shows. A psychotic break. Honorable discharge for mental illness would be the recommendation. Dowd's breaths were audible. Lou held his in. His skin crawled with energy. He sat poker straight. Still as a statue. Watching Dowd's every move and waiting for a response strangled Lou from the inside out. His fate was left in the Army's hands now. All based on an assignment he was never prepared to handle.

Dowd placed the report on the table. He straightened his demeanor.

"Interesting." Dowd left the room without another word.

Lou sat stunned into silence. He tried to interpret the meaning behind Dowd's flat tone.

We need to take action to address these ETs.

He's slipped into madness.

We need to dispose of the evidence and anyone involved.

Lou let his shoulders fall. It had happened. Whether he had wanted it to or not. He hadn't asked for it. Shit, he had wanted to avoid the call altogether. Not possible. The Army would have reprimanded him for not following orders. Lou's only job had been to take the assignment and make sure his report was painstakingly accurate. The rest was up to the authorities in the military.

Possibly in the universe.

After ruminating over worst-case scenarios and sweating through his uniform for a good half hour, the door behind Lou creaked open again. He revolved in his chair to see who it was. A woman in a tailored black dress stood in the doorway. She peered through her thick glasses, examining the clipboard in her firm grip.

"Any update on my report?"

"I have it right here."

The woman put the report along with a pen down on the table in front of him. She pointed her sparkly red manicured nail to the signature line and tapped the page. Her raised eyebrows warned him not to give him any trouble.

"You'll need to sign on this line before the Army excuses you this evening."

Lou read over the typed report. It made no mention of an unidentified flying object or a crash site. None of the details he had painstakingly described were present. The report was unrecognizable. He shook his head. The papers fluttered as he tried to hand them back to the woman.

"I'm sorry, miss. There must be a mistake. This isn't my report."

She pushed his hand away and back down on the table in front of him. The papers were still in his grip. After shoving the pen in his hand, she forced it onto the signature line of the document and huffed.

"You aren't listening, Major. Didn't they teach you to obey orders all the way back in boot camp? Sheesh. This is the formal report the Army has agreed to put on record. The one you'll attest to with your signature."

He didn't have a choice. Not when it came to the Army. Pressing his pen to the signature line, he slowly signed his name with a shaky hand. Rat bastards. Lou was unsettled. He needed to know what the Army would do with their authentic testimonials.

"I trust you have put the original reports in the proper hands?"

The woman snatched the signed document. She promptly retrieved her pen.

"That's top secret, Major. You know better than to ask me classified questions."

"The content is mine. It's far from top secret to me."

"You experienced a false alarm, just like your acknowledged report states."

"Forget that report. I want to know what happened to my original account."

"Enough with the silly talk. We're done here. You're excused."

The woman held the door open for Lou to exit. He stood mechanically and left the room. About halfway down the hallway on their way out, an officer Lou didn't recognize from afar summoned the woman. She raised a finger at Lou.

"I trust you know your way out."

"I do."

The woman turned on her heels and headed toward the office. Before ducking down a hallway, she slid her clipboard in a mail slot upside down. Lou spun around. No one was behind him or anywhere else. He stared at the clipboard. Taking a leap of faith, he slid toward the mailboxes trying not to make a sound. He pulled out the clipboard and flipped it over. A bolded stamp stared back at him.

RESTRICTED.
TOP SECRET/SPECIAL CLEARANCE EYES ONLY.

He scanned the hallway one last time. No one was there to catch him. In a rush, he yanked the document from the pile. He quickly crumpled it in his palm. Heat coursed through his veins. Rollins put his hand next to his pants. He slid it into his pocket. His fingers opened until the document separated from him. He gently slid his hand out from the pocket and pressed it against the outside of his pants making the stolen classified document blend with the wrinkle in his polyester.

Once in his car, Lou carefully opened the document. He read it in its entirety under the dim interior lights. He began to tremble from the inside out.

CHAPTER TWELVE

MARCI'S TRUCK screeched to a hard stop in her driveway right before almost hitting Lou's protruding belly. She was eager to research a few more topics on the evidence NASA released, then publish her blog post on *Among Us*. Plans had changed. For the better, she hoped. She twisted the key out of the ignition, grabbed her purse, and hopped out of her truck.

"Just the person I wanted to see."

He scanned Cedar Lane behind her. "I figured you'd be home right after the news broke. Okay if I come in?"

"You owe me a surprise visit after I practically broke down your door this morning."

Marci turned around. No one was there. She pressed the code to open her front door. She forced a laugh, trying to make light of the heaviness between them. The air was as thick as mud. She pushed opened the door and led her old neighbor into the kitchen as she dismantled the alarm. Despite its more modern decor, it was the identical layout as in Lou's house across the street. She wanted his opinion on everything that had transpired that afternoon.

"Peppermint tea?"

"Whiskey."

Marci wasn't surprised he had asked. Lou loved his whiskey. If ever there was a time to day drink, it was now. She grabbed his favorite Irish jug from the dining room cabinet and dropped it on the counter. If he was drinking, so was she. Marci poured their drinks into the proper glassware. She sat down across from her neighbor at the small bistro table and slid the whiskey to Lou.

"It's never too early for booze." Marci clinked her glass with her old neighbor.

"Amen."

Lou took more than a small taste. Half of the drink was gone when he put the glass down. The two neighbors had a history of discussing their theories on the universe, including the existence of aliens, for hours on end. He was a believer like Marci. It was one of the many reasons they had connected and become fast friends. They spent many sleepless nights on her porch marveling over the vast evening sky. With Lou a widower and Marci single, they shared a friendly, familial companionship she treasured. Marci waited for the whiskey to relax his shoulders before speaking.

"What's on your mind?"

Lou stared into the booze. "The truth. Nothing but the truth. So help me God."

Marci bit her lip. If he was going to tell her a truth related to the breaking news there had to be a reason he had kept it secret up until that point. A serious reason.

"You sure you want to do this?"

"It's time you knew everything I know."

Lou didn't look up from his drink. Marci put her hand on his. It was trembling. Marci's cheeks warmed. She was honored to have such an esteemed man of service express an obligation to her, a civilian.

"You don't owe me an explanation for anything. Some things are meant for certain ears only."

Lou's haggard expression told Marci the truth he was about to reveal had been weighing on him for some time.

"Not true. The truth is the least I can give in exchange for your friendship. Especially after what's happened to the world this week."

"My friendship is free of charge."

"Mine comes at a price. Maybe one too steep."

The old man's face twisted with conflict. Marci's insides vibrated in response. Adrenaline rushed through her veins. She fidgeted with a napkin, unable to be still. *The price of life.* Deadly or not, she needed the information Lou was withholding, for her own sanity. Curiosity would kill her if he kept silent. Recording their conversation wasn't an option, though it crossed her mind.

"It's something I need to know, isn't it?"

Lou put his forearms on the table. He leaned into their conversation.

"It's something you already know. Something you've always known. You only need the proof to back it up."

"You have proof?"

"Beyond what's been covered in the media, yes. It's been eating away at my heart for too long."

The former soldier reached into his pocket. He pulled out a piece of paper that had been neatly folded into a square. He carefully laid it on the kitchen table between their drinks. Marci's eyes glided to the words on the page stamped with a bold warning.

RESTRICTED.

TOP SECRET/SPECIAL CLEARANCE EYES ONLY.

More than enough to pique her curiosity. Her eyes darted to the next bolded phrase. The first line of a paragraph too tiny to read. Four words she had always known to be true screamed at her.

WE ARE NOT ALONE.

CHAPTER THIRTEEN

LOU WIPED his forehead with a napkin. Heart palpitations grew unstoppable. No time to breathe. His story needed to be told.

Marci poured him another glass of liquor. Lou slowly lifted it to his lips. He drank the whole damn thing in one shot.

"No rush. One word at a time."

"I might as well get right into it."

"Whenever you're ready."

Lou exhaled all the air in his lungs. His hands were trembling. Just like that day in his car at the fort. Everything was coming back to him. Everything he had worked his whole life to suppress. No need to hide the truth anymore. He recounted every moment from the night he investigated the suspected UFO crash in the nearby wetlands. Describing what he saw in important detail made him dizzy. He told her how he wrote it up in the report. How the Army changed the facts. How he attested to their statement with his lie of a signature.

"After that incident, the Army trusted me. I was given

more assignments in the ET realm, including covering up controversial cases of alien abduction. Even the famous ones the media still dissects to this day. Only a select group of us know the truth."

"I had no idea."

"How would you? We were sworn to secrecy. Expressly forbidden to ever discuss our experiences. More like threatened, if you ask me."

"I'm obsessed with those cases. We talk about them on *Among Us*. I can't believe you were privy to that level of classified information."

"And more."

"Why all the elaborate cover-ups? There's power in knowing the truth."

"The public never knew what was real or not. A lot of it was fake. The government orchestrated a good amount of the hype to distract us. The armed forces and U.S. government also knew exactly what was going to happen before any abduction took place. The Army's job was to monitor the encounter, as well as to document their report, ensuring the beings behaved as they said they would and caused no harm to the humans. Extraterrestrial beings were permitted to abduct people for all kinds of experimentation. The only caveat was the abductee needed to be returned quickly and unharmed. And most importantly, with all of their memories removed."

"Oh no." Marci was pale. And on her third glass of whiskey.

"Unfortunately, yes. As crazy as it sounds, the whole scheme went perfectly. At first. Looking back, I wish I had the balls to say something. Maybe I was too young or too eager to kiss ass and raise my rank. I'd never question my superiors back then. Even if I were brave enough, I would have been killed on the spot if I didn't obey their strict protocols."

"Murder."

"Many times."

"It's not that I'm surprised. I'm not. I just hoped I was wrong about that part."

"Far from wrong. I preferred to be on the inside of crossing that line. A man with secret and dangerous knowledge was safe. It was also sexy. Part of me thought it was a great honor and privilege to have such information, especially when it came from high ranking officials."

"You couldn't have known the consequences."

"Nope. I had no idea how it would affect the course of my entire life. It was more than a job. What I learned in the military was the catalyst for my mortality. Sharing it meant my instant death. Hiding it meant my slow, agonizing death."

"I don't know how you kept those secrets all that time."

"I played the role they needed me to play. I never agreed in my heart. What they were doing was horrific and unimaginable. Against everything I ever believed about humankind. As time went on, I got married, I had a kid. Harboring the Army's dark secrets became the only way to keep my family safe."

"I'm so sorry, Lou."

"When Irene and Eric were murdered immediately after a few of our men leaked classified information to the media, I had to change my tune entirely. The government held fast to their word. Anyone involved in top-secret alien disclosure was forced to pay the ultimate sacrifice. Leaking classified information meant sudden death. They didn't care who did the leaking. Everyone involved suffered. I'm not sure who was responsible for the leaks that took my family from me. I guess it didn't matter."

Marci's mouth fell open. Her hand flew to her chest. She stared off into the distance. Disbelief and shock painted on her expression.

"Oh, Lou. I'm so sorry. You never talked about what happened to them. I never asked because I didn't want to pry. Or upset you. In all honesty, I assumed they'd been killed in a car accident."

"I promised their souls in heaven I'd dedicate every breath I took to avenge their deaths when the time was right. That time is now."

"My heart hurts for you. What a burden to carry all those years."

"More than you know."

Lou extended his shaking hand holding the classified document across the table to meet Marci.

"For fifty years, I've harbored this document. It's been locked away in my safe waiting for the day the truth was revealed to the world. Releasing the one piece of evidence that cannot be denied is fulfilling my divine promise."

Marci tightened her grip as she took the document from Lou. "I'm speechless."

"Tough stuff, the truth. Take your time to read this thoroughly. Absorb it all. Go over it repeatedly if you need to. Digest what you learn. It details pertinent information the media will certainly leave out for fear of persecution."

"Why are you giving this to me?"

"You're the only person alive I trust with the truth. You'll know exactly what to do with it. I hope it's to tell the world."

"I can't risk your life to prove I'm not a fraud."

"You didn't go to school all those years to say things the

wrong way. You have a way with words, English professor or not. Humanity deserves to know this isn't the first time we've been visited. They need to understand why we've repeatedly been abducted, with denial from everyone involved, from reporters to government officials. Your proof is in your hands. Share it. But do so wisely."

"I'll do it for you, Lou."

Lou stood slowly. "One stipulation. Destroy the document after you read it. Shred it. Set it on fire. Whatever it takes. No one can ever find it. Ever. Don't leave any physical proof of the knowledge you're sharing behind."

"Done. Thank you for believing in me. It means everything."

"You and me, kid, we're kindred souls. Nobody can take our connection away from us."

Lou shuffled back across Cedar Lane. His head hung low. He had surrendered a hefty burden, passing the baton to Marci. It was her turn to cross the finish line. Although he doubted this race had a winner.

CHAPTER FOURTEEN

MARCI CHECKED HER WATCH. She had about fifty minutes before Ana was due to show up for work. Avoiding her boss, no longer friend, was critical. Marci wanted to save whatever face she had left. She unzipped the small roller suitcase on her desk and opened the top. No need for a cardboard box and all the dramatics accompanying a formal termination. Thank goodness. Marci packed quickly. Each item was thrown into her suitcase with haste. She wanted to be ready to wheel the bag out of her classroom at a moment's notice with all the dignity that accompanied the paid administrative leave she deserved.

Her mind was preoccupied. Rightfully so. Massive implications of posting the document she had promised to release on *Among Us* weighed on her mind. Lou had told her to destroy the record. She would. She hadn't yet. She couldn't. No one would believe her mere words. She needed to share the proof.

And undeniable proof it was.

Distracted, she logged onto *Among Us* from her phone. Her promise of releasing confidential details about a human-alien pact, a contract only someone on the inside would have been privy to, launched her blog into viral status. Within hours, Marci had gained over one million followers.

Excitement turned to fear when Marci realized the implications. If they found out who she really was, Lou would no longer be anonymous either. It wouldn't take long for the media to release the news that the blogger's neighbor was a retired Army General privy to countless abductions, Area 51, the Roswell files, and much more. Given his past confidential assignments, he had been given access to all of it, including details she would never be able to make up if she tried. Lou had been a trusted military man on the inside of the government's pact with extraterrestrial beings. The very covenant she promised to expose on *Among Us.*

Was she willing to risk her life for the truth? Lou certainly had. He lived his life like he had nothing to lose. Did she?

Staring in disbelief at her follower count as it rose exponentially by the minute, the door to her classroom creaked open. It forced her to look up. A slender, handsome man she had never seen before stood in her doorway. He wore a dark gray suit and bow tie, overdressed for her university's casual attire. His cautious demeanor coupled with the square, plastic-rimmed glasses and brown leather messenger bag told her he was out of his league.

"Ms. Simon, may I have a moment of your time?"

He carefully stepped into the room, as if waiting for her permission to enter. Marci extended her arm to shake his hand.

"Call me Marci."

He squeezed harder than anyone ever had. Marci

would typically have pulled away briskly. His hazel eyes mesmerized her into a trance.

"I'm Dr. Alton, the new professor on staff. You can call me Peter."

"Peter, it is. What do you teach?"

"Astronomy."

Marci's heart began to beat a little faster. Her colleague was not only good looking, he was also into the cosmos. Her eyes glanced down at his left hand. No wedding ring.

"Your head must be spinning after the recent news."

He squinted at her. "Not really. I stick to the facts. I'm a scientist first. The media is hardly a reliable source for objective information."

Marci's breath hitched. This was why men weren't attracted to her. Forget unlovable. She was unlikeable. Some ridiculous version of herself came out in the presence of a Y chromosome.

"Welcome to Jersey Shore University."

Peter tilted his head her way. She hadn't exited out of *Among Us*. A flush crept across her cheeks. He glanced at her oversized phone screen conveniently pointed his way.

"Are you published? I see you have a website."

"Not in the way I'd like to be. I write a blog. No biggie."

"Of course you do. You're an English professor. What's the angle? Maybe I'll check it out sometime."

Marci chuckled under her breath. She wanted to roll her eyes but held back.

"Astronomy-ish."

"A girl after my own heart."

"You're the expert. Feel free to submit a guest post any time. I can interview you."

"Mind if I look at your latest post?"

She handed Peter, a stranger, her cell phone. What was she thinking?

"Go for it."

"M.E. Simone, huh?"

"I didn't want to steer too far off course. It's not the best online disguise."

"No disguise at all."

Marci watched as Peter's eyes moved left to right across the screen. His face twisted in seriousness. Flickers of intrigue and horror crossed his expression. She was afraid to ask what he thought. Since this was his area of expertise, he would likely interject his opinion without a prompt. Professors were notorious for being didactically curious and know-it-alls. Peter seemed no different. The bowtie had said it all. He handed her phone back to her.

"You're a great writer. But you knew that already."

"I know less than you think."

"Are you really planning to publish a top-secret government document online?"

"Seems that way."

"You're in possession of this type of document?"

The hair on Marci's arms stood upright. Something wasn't sitting well with her when it came to Peter. She assumed it was discomfort over her blogging about an area where he was an expert.

"Do you really think that's safe?"

Marci took few steps backs. She distanced herself from the man she had been slightly attracted to moments ago.

"It's just a blog. It's not like I'm solving the world's problems."

"You'll be exposing something you have no business exposing." His voice was an eerie whisper lined with a warning.

If Marci was going to release this document, she had better push the envelope with this mystery man now. Time to try courage on for size.

"You're not a believer?"

"Please. Give me a little more credit. No offense, Marci. *Among Us* is pure fiction to me. Entertainment sells. I get it. It's just not my shot of bourbon."

Marci turned back to her suitcase before lashing out at him. He was not attractive. He was rude. She went back to shuffling a few items around.

"Doesn't sound like I'd be exposing much of anything."

"Headed out of town after your post goes live?"

"Why do you care what I post on the Internet?"

"Care is the wrong word. Coming from an English professor, that makes me a little nervous."

"Questioning my credentials? Maybe I should ask for yours, Dr. Alton."

"Consider my visit your own personal public service announcement from a concerned civilian. For your safety."

Marci's breathing quickened. She had been concerned, too. Peter confirming it set her on edge. She put the last of her belongings in the suitcase and zipped it closed.

"You're insinuating I'll be in danger if I post this document."

"Believer or not, we've all heard the stories. You don't mess with the government's credibility. I have my opinion. Based on fact. You'll need to be the judge for your own life."

She dropped her suitcase to the floor and extended the handle.

"I missed those stories. Why don't you fill me in?"

"The Chicago man who spotted a UFO flying over his neighborhood last month. He snapped a picture and gave it to the local paper. Two days later, he was found dead in his apartment. Accidental electrocution got him."

"I hadn't heard about it."

No way his death was related to the photograph. People talked about this stuff all the time. TV shows were created on the topic. Books—fiction and nonfiction—were published. A random man's report got him killed? A little far-fetched for Marci's taste.

"The Pittsburgh woman who uploaded a video onto a news station's website three weeks ago. Shortly after, she called in to the morning show to tell her story. She went missing after the broadcast. She's still gone."

Marci's underarms were sticky with perspiration. She wanted to fan herself but didn't want to make it obvious that she was sweating. Her only goals were to leave the classroom and get as far away from Peter as possible. She slung her purse over her shoulder. She had about fifteen minutes until she might run into Ana. That kind of discomfort was not on her agenda for any day.

"Urban legends."

"Or the truth. Where do you think that videographer who submitted the proof of that alien being is now? Or better yet, where is the NASA representative who revealed the breaking news someone who no longer has a job thought was a good idea?"

"Safe at home?"

Marci swallowed hard. She grabbed the handle of her suitcase, ready to end their conversation and roll out of the room. Peter turned to face her from the hallway.

"Think again. Ask yourself, Ms. Simon, if you're really willing to gamble with your life over a hoax."

Peter didn't give Marci a chance to respond. He disappeared into the crowd of students.

CHAPTER FIFTEEN

EXHAUSTED AFTER A TRYING DAY, Marci grabbed a glass of whiskey and her laptop. Her encounter with Peter had been more than haunting. Her last day of work for who knew how long, maybe forever, weighed heavily on her mind. She focused on a place where she held some control. And joy.

Under an hour until midnight. The time when Marci had promised to post the top-secret document from Lou. Marci had to do some last minute online research first. After Lou and Peter had both warned her, she wondered if her life was really at stake. These two overprotective men must have been exaggerating—just underestimating her ability to take care of herself. She would show them.

Marci clicked on the Internet icon on her computer. She searched the Internet for details on the stories Peter had mentioned. More like scare tactics. Propaganda not to mess with the government. More lies. Counterintelligence was more prevalent than intelligence. If those incidents occurred, someone would have leaked them to the press.

The media would have spread the news like the flu virus. Marci hadn't heard a word.

After clicking on a few links, she stumbled upon Peter's so-called news stories. Over four weeks ago, Oakwood resident Bernard Walker emailed his local newspaper with a photograph he had taken on his phone. It was a bright shot of a triangular shaped craft hovering over his home. Authorities deemed it a military aircraft. No military drills had been conducted in the area. Precisely like Peter said, two days later, Bernard's dog walker found him slumped on the floor underneath an exposed outlet. His cell phone was never recovered.

Pittsburgh native Rhonda Woodward disappeared hours after calling in to her local news station about the photograph she had sent in. According to an insider, the picture had since vanished from the news station's files. They were investigating Rhonda's disappearance as a potential homicide. Neighbors reported overhearing a violent argument between Rhonda and her fiancé earlier that same day.

Most disturbing to Marci were the latest reports. They were the reason she understood Peter and Lou's strong warnings. Local Jersey Shore videographer Ron Petro died in a car crash on the Garden State Parkway shortly after releasing the video to the public. He apparently lost control of his car and careened off a bridge into the water. While preliminary reports indicated that fellow drivers said Petro looked like he was having a seizure, another article with the 911 call transcript suggested that his brakes failed.

They had likely been cut.

Worst of all, NASA representative Michael Force had left the office right after he held an apparently unauthorized press conference regarding revealing the truth to the world.

He had told them it was to release details on a terrorist cell about to attack. A hot project he had been working on for months. Once the press conference started, they couldn't stop it. To save face, they let him run with the news.

Mr. Force never made it home.

An avid jogger found his body in the woods off I-95. Michael's head was blown off. A shotgun alongside his slumped corpse. NASA superiors released a statement retracting everything Michael said. They told the media Michael had been fired following the fake press conference. He proceeded to threaten to commit suicide knowing the truth would be leaked to the press.

Unfortunately for NASA, the bell had rung. No one bought the fake press conference story. Most people seemed to believe NASA only acted after backlash following the report proved they had made a colossal mistake in judgment.

Marci didn't have a toe, let alone a leg, to stand on. She was back to square one. Lou and Peter had been right. Every single documented report where proof surfaced that seemingly couldn't be dismissed, or evoked an implication of a government conspiracy, the person who came forward had either been the victim of untimely and accidental death or disappeared without a trace.

The blood rushed through Marci's veins. Lives had been lost. Families were left behind to forever grieve. People died. Over what? The truth? Or something worse that Marci had no business poking her nose around in.

She shut off the computer and paced her cluttered bedroom in tight circles. Marci did not want to die. That was a given. She couldn't sit idly by while the government murdered anyone who threatened to expose them. It was madness. Mayhem.

Lou had done his part and then some. She couldn't ask any more of him. Marci couldn't be the only person who believed humanity was worth saving. Others would agree. They had to be outraged at what was happening. Help was out there. She needed to find them and tell them the truth.

As if the universe was responding to her question, her phone rang. It was Marci's mom. Not exactly the person who would jump down the rabbit hole with her. More like fill the rabbit hole with concrete and block it off with armed guards.

"What's up, Ma?"

"Geez. Can't a mother call her daughter to say hi?"

"I'm in the middle of something right now. Everything okay?"

"You tell me. I was about to send the police over to make sure you were still alive. Where have you been?"

"Work. Home. The usual. What's the emergency?"

"Everything's fine. No emergency. We're worried about you. You haven't been answering your phone. We've been trying to reach you since the news report. The world has gone to hell in a handbasket. It's official."

Marci glanced at her house phone. Sixteen voicemails.

"I've been preoccupied. I told you to call my cell when you can't get me at home."

"Got your voicemail there, too."

Five more voicemails on her cell phone. "Oops."

"You eventually come home to your perfectly good, working landline. You need to check your voicemail more often. That's the problem."

Checking messages wasn't on her list of to-dos. After her mother scolded her, Marci was sure that would change. Her mom was right. Marci had no life. Her parents had retired to Florida a few years ago. Landlines were still a necessity in those areas when terrible storms and blatant lack of cell towers made broadband signals unstable at best.

"I'll get right on that."

"Anyway...did you hear the latest? NASA says a terminated staffer dreamed up the hoax for attention. That photographer was apparently bat-poop crazy. A logical explanation was inevitable."

"Don't believe everything you hear."

Her mom laughed. "You prefer I believe in UFOs."

"The media lies."

"Wait a second. You think UFOs are real? Come on. You're smarter than that, Marcella. I didn't raise you to be a pushover."

Her childhood name sent shivers down her spine.

"I don't want to fight. Let's drop the subject, Ma."

"We're not fighting. Tell me about the UFO stuff."

"I don't know what that photographer saw because I wasn't there to see it myself."

"What do you think it was?"

"I don't think we're the only living beings in the universe. If the government knows this for sure, they will do whatever they could so no one learned the truth. That's what they're doing now."

"Don't tell me you're watching those alien shows on that cable channel? Sweetie, you know they're made up for ratings. Dad could tell you stories."

"He worked on his college radio station. It's not the same thing."

"It's all entertainment. Don't let that garbage get into your head. You're a professor, not a conspiracy theorist."

"Those documents they released with the Freedom of Information Act aren't fiction."

"Have you been to church lately?"

"Church has nothing to do with it."

"I knew it. Get yourself back to Sunday Mass. Then tell me what you believe. Stop watching those darn shows. They're messing with your beautiful mind."

"Let's assume it's someone's crazy imagination. Then why is the government killing people over the release of fake information? Murder is wrong. I learned that much in church."

"There's no getting through to you. We'll talk after you go to confession."

First church, now confession? Marci rolled her eyes as if her mom was in the room and could see her.

"Fine."

"I love you. Even though your head is in the clouds."

"Love ya, Ma."

So much for her parents' moral support. Marci was pitting herself against an angry mob of elected killers. Her only backup was a seventy-plus-year-old man. She was ready to risk her life to fight for what she believed in. Bravery had nothing to do with it. Fear of living the rest of her life as a lie was her only motivation.

A few minutes left until midnight. Time to leap off the cliff with no parachute. Marci downed two shots of whiskey. A sense of calm fell over her. Her mind was more precise than it had ever been. She opened *Among Us* in administration mode. She pulled up her post page.

Marci was headed into uncharted territory. Entering the vast dark unknown was scary as hell. Ready for whatever came her way.

She held her breath for a beat. Then clicked *Publish*.

CHAPTER SIXTEEN

PIERCE JOTTED DOWN a few more notes on the almost full pad next to his computer. His checklist was created. Each step confirmed. All systems were a go. Confident he had what it took to do his job tonight, he logged out of the secret chat room. The most elite group of underground hackers in all North America frequented the virtual meeting place. They had spent months training Pierce on how to gain unauthorized access to anything he wanted on the dark web. Navigating the online underground with the best of the worst cybercriminals pumped his blood like a shiatsu massage. The ESA agent's latest hobby was diving into bad sites and getting into as much trouble as he could online. Hours after Lindsay's head hit the pillow, Pierce used his all-access pass to do some damage in the web's underworld.

All those hours hadn't changed the fact that Pierce's hacking skills were subpar compared to agents who had been at it for years. His skills were decent. He was no subject matter expert. When he couldn't risk even the slightest misstep, Miles was on speed dial. His go-to Internet-delinquent partner would take over and complete the job at a moment's notice.

Miles hung on Pierce's speakerphone. He needed his partner for support tonight in case things went south. His assignment to hack into *Among Us* required perfect execution. Any errors in the mission could be globally catastrophic.

He clicked on a few prompts then entered a code. His computer screen cycled through several images before asking to share his screen with Miles. Over the next few minutes, they worked side by side to break into *Among Us* and Marci's laptop simultaneously. Once in, it was as if they were sitting in her office chair themselves.

"Looks like she logged on about twenty minutes ago. She hasn't done anything since then," Pierce said.

"Her history shows it takes her about a half hour to get going. We wait. No need to shut it down and raise red flags if she's going to chicken out," Miles said.

Pierce sipped bourbon on the rocks as he waited for Marci to do something. Anything.

"I don't know if my scare tactics worked. She's a bit of a pain in the ass. Headstrong."

"She'll learn about reality soon enough. Lou certainly didn't slow her down. She published that post right after she left his house."

"Whatever he said lit a fire under her ass. In the wrong direction," Pierce said.

"We'll amp up pressure on him. It wasn't only Marci. They both witnessed those bastards."

"First things first. Shut down her Internet tonight. Take drastic action tomorrow."

Pierce wasn't ready to harm Marci. At least not until necessary. He liked her, even though he shouldn't. Maybe a little too much. He had no idea why. It wasn't because she was outright beautiful. She wasn't. Average looking women never grabbed his attention. He favored lookers like his Lindsay. Marci was special, though. Something about her drew him close. Her passion for the unknown. Her drive. The energy she exuded. Smart. Tough. Undeterred.

Guilt swarmed over him. He had no business liking anyone. Especially not Marci. He was a married man. She was the enemy. He had to remind himself of those facts. They disturbed him on several levels.

Miles caught Pierce's attention. "Heads up. She's on."

Pierce worked on disabling *Among Us*. Miles managed to take over Marci's computer. Pierce watched partially in shock at how Marci was so blatantly willing to release confidential information to the public. It was the last thing anyone who knew the truth would ever want to do. Even the most educated and evolved civilians couldn't handle the truth. Not even a slight implication of it.

Marci plummeted headfirst into a danger zone. It might cost her everything. To save the data, and perhaps Marci's life, Pierce had only one thing to do next. At the precise moment the laptop camera showed Marci about to press *Publish*, Pierce hit *Delete*. Simultaneously, Miles crashed her computer. They exhaled in unison. It sounded like a gust of wind.

"Mission accomplished." Pierce took another swig of his bourbon.

"For now. This is just the beginning."

"I appreciate your help, my brother. I've got this from here."

"I don't think so. I won't allow you to take on such a groundbreaking case alone. I'll be at your condo in New Jersey at eight o'clock tomorrow morning."

"Nonsense. I won't have it. Your wife is pregnant. The last thing you need is to put your life in any more danger than it already is. I'll reach out when a consult is needed. That's what partners do."

"Beth can handle herself. It's our fourth kid. At this point, we're practically raising a pack. So long as I'm there for the delivery, she won't kill me."

"She's not the murderer I'm worried about."

"Let them hack me up into bits. The ESA's five million dollar life insurance policy will have to cover Beth and the kids. She might even be better off. On second thought, don't dare tell her how much I'm worth dead. She will kill me herself."

"I get it. ESA resume builder."

"Can't hurt. While you're closing in on Marci, I'll hijack Lou. Tag team. Like the old days."

Pierce was being micromanaged. Worse. His partner wanted to babysit him. He could handle Marci Simon all on his own. He had been trained for more difficult scenarios than an English professor-turned-blogger threatening them with a piece of fifty-year-old paper. He would run circles around her case if Miles would just stay out of his way. A cog in the wheel was the last thing anyone needed.

What Pierce didn't want to admit to anyone, including himself, was that he was genuinely worried for Marci's safety with Miles around. A great partner in the ESA also meant a sociopathic, brutal killer. Any wrong moves on Marci's part would end in her death. No hesitation. No mercy. Pierce couldn't fight on this one. He had no choice but to open his doors to the ESA's version of the criminally insane.

"I'll put the coffee on, dear."

"Add ammo to mine."

"Gunpowder it is."

He let out a huge breath. They had thwarted Marci's plan. Temporarily. If she was in possession of the document, she was a threat to national security. She needed to be watched. Controlled. Possibly terminated. He didn't want it to come to that, but his job came first. His career was more important than anything. Even the loss of innocent lives.

Sitting in a chair by the window overlooking the Atlantic Ocean, Pierce drank his bourbon slowly. Every sip savored. He stared into the night sky. He knew more than he had ever wanted to know when he started out as a young and hungry rookie agent. Truths that had leveled presidents, both emotionally and figuratively, hadn't taken Pierce down. The reality of life on Earth was destined to shock the world. Destroying any hope for global peace. Start epic world wars. Wars designed to end lives.

Imminent extinction of humanity.

The truth about the universe was Pierce's blessing. His burden. Humanity's curse. If he didn't have the power to change it, the least he could do was become the force to protect those who didn't know they needed protection.

He was their savior under the government's disguise of a cold-blooded killer.

CHAPTER SEVENTEEN

THE INFAMOUS BLUE and gray screen of death screamed at Marci. Her heart sank to her feet. Her computer had crashed. Maybe it was just the Internet. Spinning around to check the wireless router, all the bright green lights were on. Every single one of them.

Chills raced through her veins. Her hands shook as she pressed the button to shut her computer down. It wasn't a fluke.

They knew about the post.

They were after the document.

Confirmed a target, she refused to give up now. As soon as the computer noise completely disappeared, she rebooted it. It took longer than she wanted. Her laptop was ancient. She didn't make enough money to invest in a new one. Especially not after being fired from her job. When it got back online, it just sat there. Nothing appeared on the screen. She punched her desk. At the worst time, everything had turned its back on her.

Plan B.

She pulled out her cell and used her fingerprint to open

the screen. It was the one safety feature she was thankful for now. No one could replicate her print. Except for the government. They could do anything they wanted.

The lock screen on her phone disappeared. She breathed a sigh of relief. She had overreacted. Again. Her shitty old computer died. Instead of accepting that, she brazenly jumped to the conclusion she was on the CIA's hit list. Ridiculous. She needed to get a grip.

Marci clicked on an icon on her phone's main screen. The shortcut took her straight to *Among Us*. It was gone.

HTTP ERROR 404 (NOT FOUND)

She stared in disbelief. This could not be happening. All her worst fears were coming to life. The infancy of a panic attack loomed. Heart beating out of her chest. Choking sensation. Numbness crawling over her face. A few deep breaths did nothing. Calming herself was the only escape. If she lost it, she would never get through what she needed to do next.

After her shoulders fell an inch, Marci dove right in. Wasting no time, she clicked on the web address line. Ignoring the lingering anxiety, she retyped the address for *Among Us*. This time, she verified every keystroke. Sometimes the Internet changed the address to automatically visit an *https* site. *Among Us* was not secure. Something she needed to change ASAP.

She double-checked her entry and hit *Go*.

HTTP ERROR 404 (NOT FOUND)

Marci's intense shaking returned. Full-blown panic mode. She was sure she had renewed her domain name and web service months ago. If there were an error with her payment, she would have been notified.

Among Us had disappeared. Another government casualty.

Nausea swirled in her gut. *Among Us* hadn't vanished accidentally. Marci and *Among Us* had been personally attacked. A semi-innocent attack. For now. Maybe even a warning. If she didn't take their hint, there would be more.

Worse.

Whoever had hacked into her Wi-Fi and computer could have put a tap on her phone. Audio recorders and cameras might even be planted around her house. Her car. Anywhere. Everywhere. To act, Marci had to use as little advanced technology as possible. She needed to secure the classified document they refused to allow her to release.

Marci unlocked the filing cabinet under her desk. She pulled open the drawer. Reaching her hand into the very last file in the back, she retrieved a zipped folder. It contained the valuable, irreplaceable paper. Forget the shaking. Marci's entire arm rocked back and forth now. Men and women from all over the world had sacrificed their lives to protect the secrets she was about to reveal. Marci would whack their cover through the ozone layer.

She surveyed the room. Missing a fly on the wall would be the death of her. "Men in black" came in all forms. Scrutinizing as much as she reasonably could, she was sure she was alone. Never too safe. Always on guard.

Marci unzipped the file. She systematically slipped the document out of the envelope. Her hands trembled uncontrollably. The paper jumped in response. She would have been mortified if anyone was watching her. Fear consumed her entire body. She could barely breathe. She didn't let it stop her. Her nerves were on a high. Unruly and wild.

No turning back. Ever.

Marci's next steps meant life or death. Lou and Peter had warned her. She chose to ignore them. The evidence was there in plain sight. She was fully aware of what she was getting into. Only now, she was on the receiving end. Her life was in danger. A hint tonight. A hunt tomorrow. The prospect both terrified and excited her.

Marci's life up until that point had been a dull jumble of ways to be who everyone else wanted her to be. She hid behind her education all her life. Smothering her true self before *Among Us* came along and turned the light on in her heart. She finally understood why her passion for exploring the unknown had pushed her to write such a blog.

Purpose. Marci had a goal in life. Something to believe in. A cause to fight for. No matter the danger, she was finally living.

Marci was on a mission. Her mind was made up. Carrying her dream out to fruition was the next step. What did she have to lose?

Everything.

Nothing at all.

Her hands stopped trembling. Her nerves calmed. Quiet confidence stirred inside of her. She stood from her desk and headed to the closet. On the top shelf, hidden under boxes of papers she had no idea why she saved, was an old laptop. She didn't need the Internet. A scanner and a flash drive would work perfectly fine. No wireless Internet. No access to her worn-out computer. Technology had been the death of privacy. And life.

Let them come for her. They would eventually get her. When they did, they would need to do a better job than merely securing an old government document. Marci had zero plans to let the one piece of precious information slip out of her hands and away from those who needed to know its contents the most. The public had been living in a media fog, brainwashed for the last hundred years. All of that was about to change on a dime.

If Marci was the sacrificial lamb, then so be it. Someone had to do it. As far as she could tell, no one else was stepping up to the plate. It was her destiny. She was born to tell this truth. Her purpose was crystal clear. After too many years of walking unconsciously through life, going through the motions, living in that same fog, Marci was alive. She had a mission. Tell the world everything.

She had known it since her childhood. Visitations, she was told, were her wild imagination. Bringing her creativity into reality. It was a form of dreaming. Hallucinating. Bullshit.

A truth she confirmed with the spaceship sighting. Further validated with the NASA report. Solidified with Lou's document. A reason had to exist that all those things had happened to her. A reason she bought the house across the street from the man who would have the very information she needed to do what she was about to do. It was all leading up to this moment and the decisions she was about to make now.

Marci was about to end it all.

CHAPTER EIGHTEEN

THE BLARING BEEPING from the smoke alarm woke Lou from a sound sleep. He jumped up out of his bed, startled. His heart raced. His first thought was to get Irene and Eric out of the house. Then he remembered they had been gone for years. Lou's heart sunk like it did every time he forgot three had become one. Who cared if he lived or died? No one. He was an old and lonely man.

Survival was a nagging bitch. She forced you to save your own life even if you wouldn't mind being dead and buried six feet under. Even if you were asking your heart to stop.

A faint smell of smoke wafted into his bedroom. Lou might have been hallucinating. Or still in a dream. He couldn't be sure. He didn't trust his mind any more than he could trust his whiskey addiction.

Lou relaxed his body forcefully, exactly like they had taught him in the Army. You never forgot how to stay alive. An anxiety attack when you were under physical attack wasn't ideal. Deep breaths led to strong mental acumen.

Continuation of one's existence depended on a healthy mind. Lou was screwed.

Old batteries were the culprits. Lou was certain. He was terrible at replacing the damn smoke alarm's batteries. Those dollar store brands only lasted thirty days, if that. Stupid, because he had a good pension. A General's pension. He could afford brand-name batteries. He made a mental note to order them the next time he had his groceries delivered.

Lou rubbed his eyes. The beeping was incessant. He didn't even bother to turn on the bedroom light. He eyes wouldn't adjust that quickly anyway.

He pushed open his bedroom door to the hallway. The smell of smoke was stronger, although not as convincing as it should have been for a real fire. An investigation was in order regardless. The beeping, no longer a priority, became nothing more than background noise.

Before Lou made it to the stairs, a hand came seemingly out of nowhere and landed on his chest. It stopped him mid-step. His first reaction was to jump back. He sprang forward to attack. Another arm flew at him, connecting with his chest. A much younger, more substantial arm stopped him in his tracks.

"General Rollins. Haven't you learned your lesson?"

Lou adjusted his eyes. He blinked several times to get a clear picture of the beast before him. Dim moonlight streamed in through the small foyer window. It barely illuminated the man's face. No matter. Lou immediately understood what was happening. Nearly seven feet tall, a brooding man wearing a tailored suit and military grade buzz cut loomed. The hairstyle hadn't changed in over fifty years. Lou swore they let special agents look like civilians these days. Hardcore.

"I'd ask you how you got in, but then again you don't play by the rules." Lou stepped back a few feet to gain his composure.

"I could say the same thing about you, General."

The menacing man hovered over Lou. He peered into his eyes, searing maleficence into Lou's soul. Even in the dark, Lou's heart thumped a few extra beats. He swallowed hard.

"I learned from the very best. Just like you did."

The special agent's face was twisted. Lou had given it back to him. He didn't like it. He began to sniff obnoxiously.

"Smell any smoke? Or is it just your imagination?"

Evidence of the smoke was more than an aroma. It billowed around the corner and flew up the stairs until it hit Lou's face. His limbs began to shake. Dizziness took hold. He tried to shove past the man. The burly special agent stopped him dead in his tracks.

"You're not going anywhere."

"Get out of the way. My house is on fire."

"Precisely."

The man pushed Lou with so much force he flew back. He slid across the hallway hardwood until his back almost reached the end of the hall. Lou attempted to get his bearings. He was entirely out of sorts. His life was in danger. Haze clouded his thinking. His mind went to a faraway place.

Death might be a relief. He would be reunited with his beloved family again. It wasn't time. His hands began to tremble. Unadulterated dread engulfed him. He glared at the man who was trying to murder him. The Agency wouldn't win this time. Lou wasn't about to die by homicide. Not some illness or accident. A murderer who stood for everything Lou stood against. Lies and the ultimate disregard for human life.

It took everything Lou had to pull himself up to standing. His back was writhing in pain. He could feel the bruises forming. He forced himself upright in principle alone. No sooner did he clear his vision to see ahead again than the dishonorable man was standing right in front of him. Charcoal-gray billowing smoke was making its way into the upstairs hallway now. Heavy, breathless clouds. The fire traveled faster than hell. They didn't have much time. Lou's lungs began to hurt. He gasped for oxygen. None existed. It felt like the altitude sickness he had in the Rocky Mountains of Colorado years ago. Nothing was getting into his lungs. Time was running out for him.

"What do you want from me?"

Lou coughed out a response. His lungs were in severe pain. Pressure on his chest and back increased to unbearable. Choking on what was left of the air around him, Lou slowed his breathing to a minimum. He wasn't ready to die. Not yet.

"Send Marci a message. Think you can do that for me?"

"Leave Marci alone. She has nothing to do with anything."

The man chuckled. "Oh, you're wrong. She has everything to do with all of it."

"Any issues you have, take them out on me."

Lou coughed and wheezed, searching for any sign of oxygen. No luck. A sinister laugh emanated from the darkness.

"My only issue is Marci. She has something I want. She knows too much. If she doesn't play her cards right, she'll be part of our Termination Project. You know all about that, don't you, General Rollins?"

Images flashed in Lou's mind. Innocent lives were taken for the sake of privacy. The termination was death. When you knew too much and you didn't cooperate, you simply disappeared.

"Take my life. Leave Marci alone."

"That would be too easy."

The man's fifty-thousand-dollar smile was eerier than any government document. Lou wondered if he was even human. He would never know.

"Add a body to your count. Isn't that what you want? You'll get a bonus for taking out an enemy of the Agency."

"Yeah, but it's a ton more fun to terrorize the shit out of you. I didn't come all the way from DC to merely kill you. At least not yet. I need answers. I need what Marci has. What you gave to her."

"I don't know what you're talking about."

"You're a funny man, Louie. Real funny."

He grabbed Lou by the neck and lifted him off the ground. Lou gasped for air, choking on his tongue. Losing breath was bad enough. Now he was being choked

"You have twenty-four hours to turn the evidence over to us or convince Marci to do it. If I don't have the classified document in my cold palms within twenty-three hours, fifty-nine minutes and forty seconds from now, not only will I not show you mercy, I'll torture Marci until the ESA in DC can hear her screams. Then I'll torture her some more. Understood?"

The man slammed Lou to the ground like a bottle he was trying to break. The oxygen was completely gone now. Lou was losing consciousness, fading in and out.

The man's words reverberated through his house. "And not a second more."

Lou gasped for his last breath and collapsed.

CHAPTER NINETEEN

MARCI HAD NEVER HELD Lou's hand before.

Never got so close to anyone except maybe her mom and dad. The old man had tubes coming out of everywhere. He was hooked up to IVs, oxygen, and God only knew what other machines. Marci's heart ached. Tears welled up in her eyes. She blinked them back and kept her composure somehow. Being so emotional hadn't been natural for Marci. She couldn't help it this time. Lou had been a staple in her life since she moved onto her quiet little cul-de-sac. She only saw her parents a few times a year anymore. Lou was her local family. The best friend she ever had.

The old man opened his eyes barely enough to spot Marci. She pulled herself together for his sake. The truth was that he was okay. He was going to be okay anyway. He had suffered some smoke inhalation. She knew this because she had lied when she told the doctors that Lou was her grandfather. It's not like they asked for proof of that kind of thing. Besides, Lou had no family. At least nobody he ever talked about to her. She would be happy to step in and fill that void as he had for her so many times over the years.

That fire damn near could have killed him. No. It would have killed him if Marci hadn't seen the flames and called 911. Damage to his house was far worse than to Lou.

Lou cleared his throat. "Where am I?"

"You had a little accident."

She squeezed his hand, and he stiffened it before relaxing. The general wasn't typically warm and fuzzy, but under the steel facade he was a teddy bear.

"What happened?"

"You had a fire on the first floor of your house. You collapsed. You're going to be okay."

He squinted his eyes as if remembering something. They quickly grew wide like he was afraid of something. He coughed a few times as if he was getting himself ready to speak. He cleared his throat.

"Not an accident."

It took Marci a minute to understand what he was saying.

"I'll make this stop. I'll handle it. Don't worry. All you need to do is get better."

Lou tried to push himself up into a sitting position. Marci handed him the bed remote instead. He moved the bed until he was upright. He reached for the water on his tray table. Marci put the glass to his mouth. He took a sip and cleared his throat again.

"You can't do that. They're coming for me. And for you. Don't waste your time trying to stop them."

A nurse came into the room to take his blood pressure. Lou stopped the conversation abruptly. Marci slid her chair away to let them check him out.

"Any idea when he'll be released?"

"That's up to the doctor, honey. He's doing really well for a man his age." She took the blood pressure monitor off his arm. "You know what they say, seventy is the new forty."

"Estimate? One week? A month?"

Marci was reaching. She wanted to know how much time she had to do what she had to do while Lou was unharmed in his bed. He couldn't go home when he was released. Marci was fully prepared to let him stay with her.

"I'd say at least a week or two. Your grandfather needs to heal. He needs his rest." She pushed the medical cart to the doorway. "He's in good hands. We'll keep you posted."

The nurse disappeared into the hallway.

"...Hours," Lou said under his breath.

"I missed that." Marci leaned into him.

"Twenty-four hours. Less now."

"What's in twenty-four hours?"

"Our deadline."

"What meds do they have you on? I'm going to tell them they need to lower the dose. I think you're hallucinating."

A deep growl emerged from Lou that made Marci jump. Lou waved his hand for her to come closer.

"Listen to me. This wasn't an accident. An agent paid me a visit. He did this. He'll kill me. He'll kill you if you don't hand over that document within twenty-four hours from when I collapsed."

"Who did this to you?"

"They have a way of letting you know. Trust me."

Lou's voice was getting hoarse again. Marci gave him some more water.

"Take it easy."

"They'll come after me first. It will give you enough time to release that document to the public. Rally support on your blog, but don't release it there. Get it into the right hands."

"What hands?"

"Media. My nephew in Arlington is a state trooper. He'll understand. And help. Look him up. His name is Trent...Rollins."

"You never mentioned him before."

"Trent's father and I had a falling out years ago. Trent was only a kid. My stubborn and selfish bastard of a brother wouldn't let me have a relationship with my only nephew. I've tried to keep in touch with him after his dad died. He's busy. I never wanted to push myself on him. I didn't want him to feel like he needed to take care of an old uncle who had nobody else."

Marci's heart sank again. "Don't ever say that again. You have me. Always will."

Lou broke a smile out of his tough demeanor. "Find Trent. He'll help while I'm holed up here like a prisoner."

Marci did something she never expected. She kissed Lou on the forehead.

"You get better, old man. You hear me?"

He blushed, and his shoulders fell a bit. "Don't get yourself killed."

"Never."

Marci made her way out of the hospital. Finding Trent Rollins was the only thing on her mind. When she passed Peter in the parking lot, she almost didn't recognize him.

"Marci? Is that you? Everything all right?"

"I could ask you the same question. What are you doing here?"

"Blood work."

On the weekend? "Visiting a friend."

"I hope your friend is okay."

"He's going to be."

"Great. See you at work."

Peter rushed into his Honda and drove off. Marci followed close behind.

CHAPTER TWENTY

PIERCE GLANCED in his rearview mirror. Marci was two cars behind him. He pressed the phone button on his steering wheel, choosing the speed dial for Miles using the Bluetooth.

"She's on my tail."

"No shit. This isn't my first rodeo, brother. Now remember...go to the diner. Get a seat at the bar. She'll probably get a table somewhere in the back to watch you. I'll roll up in my black suit, all formal, exuding charm and terror like I do best. I'll make some threatening gestures. You'll look defeated. She'll come to the rescue. The perfect recipe for Ms. Simon to become your ally. One step closer to getting that document."

"That's the plan."

Pierce pressed the button to end the call. He turned down a side street into a populated area near where Marci lived. He parked in the lot for the locals' favorite diner on the main road behind her house. Marci had plenty of places to park. Either way, she would be hidden in the weekend brunch crowd. Perfect situation for Pierce. He watched everything Marci did in the diner's mirror behind the bar. Marci did exactly what Miles said she would. Ten minutes later, like clockwork, Miles took a seat next to Pierce.

Miles summoned the server. He adjusted himself on the round stool.

"Old man's alive. He got our message."

"I checked on him. He'll be out of our hair for a week or two. Marci's on the move. We need to stop her."

"We? That's all you. I have the Agency to please and Lou to handle."

He put his arm around Pierce and pulled tight.

"Figure of speech."

It wasn't. Pierce understood his orders. But Marci wasn't someone he wanted to terminate. Not now. Not ever. He would if duty called for it. After Miles downed his coffee, he shook Pierce in an aggressive gesture.

"Get that document. I don't care how. We have under a day. If we don't produce it, the Agency is coming after us personally. They won't tolerate a civilian running around with classified information."

The mission was all too clear to Pierce again. His compassion for Marci went out the window with Miles's words. Global security was at risk. Human lives were at stake. He didn't want her to die, but for the sake of humankind, one life was a small price to pay.

"Consider it done."

Miles left abruptly. Pierce watched as Marci's expression seemed to waver between getting up and staying put. He wasn't sure if Miles did enough to convince her. Pierce took it upon himself to walk by her booth on the way to the restrooms. He put on his most desperate demeanor. Slumped shoulders. Head bowed down to the floor. He pretended the world had fallen apart around him. It worked.

"Peter?" Marci's arm stopped him from walking past her.

"Hey, Marci. How's it going?"

"Fine. I'm just getting some breakfast before I run my errands today. Is everything all right?"

He feigned confusion. "All is good."

Marci looked down and then back up at Pierce. "I don't mean to pry, but I couldn't help but notice you at the bar earlier. That man, in the suit...are you sure everything is okay?"

He was in. Pierce questioned Marci with his eyes, gesturing if he could sit down for a minute.

"Do you mind?"

She waved her approval. "Sit."

Pierce shook his head in disbelief. He played with the extra set of utensils as he spoke, nervousness emanating from him. At least he hoped.

"Not too good, if I'm honest. I had no idea who that man was when he sat down. Startled the hell out of me. He told me the government sent him."

Marci's eyes grew two sizes larger. "For what reason?"

"That's what I asked him. He told me about a global security breach at Jersey Shore University. Someone on staff was harboring classified government information. At first I had no idea what he was talking about. Then I thought of..."

"Of me. You thought of me."

"I'm sorry. I didn't mean to spring all of this on you. I was trying to figure out what to do next."

"You told him about my blog."

All the color drained from Marci's face. Pierce wanted to do a happy dance. He fidgeted instead.

"We need to do something. The man told me I had to convince you to turn in the information you claimed to have. If you don't, he'll kill me."

"He actually said he would kill you?"

Pierce straightened. "He's not strong-arming me. If you don't do something, the government isn't the only group of people who are going to be after you."

She began to tremble. The fork in her hand, previously still, began to shake. Pierce couldn't watch her. He had to look away. Yet it was his job to increase the pressure on Marci. It wasn't merely the government. It was the ESA. They were deadlier than any government agency known to man. No one even knew they existed. They had free reign. Nothing was off limits. They wouldn't just kill Marci. They would kill her entire family and anyone who ever knew her. They would destroy anyone and anything in their path to get what they wanted. They wanted that document.

"I'll take care of it. No need to get involved. It's too dangerous."

"I'm in."

"No way. This is my problem to solve. You have nothing to do with this. Except that you took a job at the wrong school."

"I insist. How can I help?"

Marci bit her lip. "Ever been to Arlington, Virginia?"

That was right in his backyard. "I'll drive."

CHAPTER TWENTY-ONE

MARCI AND PETER pulled up to a sprawling artisan home on a lot five times the size of Marci's little plot of land. The borderline multi-level mansion was far above her expectations for a Virginia state trooper's residence. She had no idea what he made for a living, or what he had in his bank account, but his house impressed her.

Even after a long four-hour drive, Marci had boatloads of energy. Her nerves never let her down. She had spent the time on the road practicing the conversation with Trent in her head. Now that they were practically on his doorstep, all her confidence evaporated in the wind.

Peter parked on the street in front of Trent's house. The oversized driveway was empty. Marci had no idea if the trooper was home. She expected to see a patrol car parked nearby. Part of her was relieved. Maybe it wouldn't work out just yet. She needed more time to sort out her thoughts. They could come back later. She didn't want to. They had traveled so far. She had plenty of time to build up her courage. Both of them were eager to meet Trent right away.

"Ready?" Peter asked.

"I've been ready since you put the car in drive."

They stood on the doorstep. Peter's hands cupped the glass panels framing the double doors. Marci thought it was rude. She didn't know him well enough to say so. She summoned the courage to ring the doorbell. His house and the surrounding neighborhood were quiet. It was a sunny and warm day in Arlington, but no one seemed to be out. Marci thought it odd. A community like that should have kids running around. Women gardening. Men mowing lawns. Life.

Without warning, the door opened wide. Trent stood over six feet, broad-shouldered and muscular. Marci gasped a bit when her eyes caught his, a striking grayish blue. His military-style haircut and exercise attire told her he was serious, even when he wasn't working.

"Can I help you?" Trent looked annoyed.

"I sure hope so. I'm Marci Simon, a friend and neighbor of your Uncle Lou." She turned to her side. "This is my friend, Peter, who drove me here."

"A pleasure to meet you," Peter said.

Trent nodded. "Is Uncle Lou all right?"

Marci looked at her feet first, then back at Trent's crystalline eyes. His face fell a bit.

"Lou's okay. We wanted to talk to you about him. And some other things. He actually sent us here."

Marci tried to look beyond Trent to find out if anyone else was there with him. His oversized muscular frame was large enough to block most of her view into his house.

"I'm surprised he didn't just call me."

"I know it seems odd, but I promise I can explain. Do you mind if we come in?"

Trent hesitated. "If Uncle Lou sent you, it must be important."

He stepped out of the way to let them in. Trent gestured for them to sit at the round glass kitchen table overlooking a bay window to a sprawling, immaculately maintained backyard. The foyer alone was gorgeous with cathedral ceilings, an enormous curved staircase, and a breathy open floor plan. It was her dream home. Even though she hadn't known it before she arrived.

"Sweet tea? Coffee?" Trent asked as he headed into the granite-covered kitchen.

"Tea would be great. Thanks." Marci made herself comfortable at the table.

"Coffee for me," Peter said.

Trent poured the drinks, taking a sweet tea for himself. He sat with them at the table.

"I lost touch with Uncle Lou about a year ago. Life got busy. I feel terrible. I think about him all the time. How is he?"

Marci swallowed. "Right now, he could be better. He's in the hospital being treated for smoke inhalation. He had a fire in his house."

Trent grabbed the edge of the table with force. "Did he leave the stove on? I should have moved him down here with me."

"No, nothing like that. The first floor is pretty messed up. It needs some work. Lou was on the second floor when it happened. It had nothing to do with the stove."

Peter chimed in. "We think the government is behind his house fire. Does that mean anything to you?"

Trent squinted, looking suspicious of Peter. "Excuse me?"

Marci softened the accusation. "I know this all seems a bit crazy. Your uncle shared something private with me from when he was in the Army. It's shocking information. I think—we think—the government is after us for it."

"Something is definitely going on. Lou told her you could help."

Trent stared down Peter. "Have you ever met my Uncle Lou?"

Peter cleared his throat. "Not personally. But Marci speaks highly of him."

"How long have you known Marci?"

Trent seemed to be interviewing Peter. Marci wasn't sure why.

"Peter's a fellow professor. I teach English. He teaches astronomy."

Trent seemed to consider this information before responding.

"I don't know how I can help you two. It seems like you know more than I do."

"Maybe. I can share it with you. And you can gather whatever resources you have."

"I'm a law enforcement officer. I have no idea how I can go up against the government. I don't get hazardous pay for trying to sabotage the people who sign my paycheck. Sorry, guys. I wish I could help."

Trent stood as if to say it was time for them to go.

"Your uncle believes you can help us. I believe in Lou and everything he's shared with me from the crazy to the insane. They're after him, Trent. I think they're after me, too. I know you don't care about that because you don't know me, but if there's anything you can do to save your uncle's life, I'll take it."

"We didn't drive from New Jersey to get rejected." Peter puffed his chest out.

"Again, I'm sorry. That's not my problem. You're the

ones who decided to blindside me. Marci, I appreciate that you're loyal to my uncle. But like I said, I really don't know what I can do to help."

A photograph caught Marci's eye. It was of two people clanging beers at a bar. The person next to Trent looked oddly familiar. Marci got up from her seat and made her way to the frame. She picked up the photo without thinking and stared at the picture. His identity hit her like a freight train.

"You know Sam Chancellor?"

"Yea. We went to college together."

Peter squinted. "CNN's Sam Chancellor?"

"I figured out a way you can help us."

CHAPTER TWENTY-TWO

PIERCE'S PHONE buzzed in his pocket. He excused himself. He took a short walk down the street while Marci finished up with Trent. Pierce answered the phone. Papers rustled. Objects banged around.

"While you're vacationing in Virginia with Nancy Drew, I'm over here trying to make sense of an office organized by a neat freak." Annoyance lined Miles's voice.

"What's the verdict?"

"Jury's still out. Nothing stored here. At least not that I can find alone. I'm taking her laptop for forensic analysis."

"Put everything back in its place.

"It'll all be back on her pretty little perfect desk before you're back in Jersey."

"She can't know you were there."

"Let me do my job. Find that document like you promised. I don't care if it's paper, electronic, or a psychic connection. The ESA's bomb ticker is going down."

"You're helping me. This is my case. I'm not your assistant."

Miles laughed. "Whatever you say. It's your case.

Except the ESA's all over my ass to keep an eye on you. I'd say it was the Agency's case. You know best."

The Agency sent him? "Keep it clean. I'll handle Marci."

"I'm running out of time to deliver something to the Agency. A document or a person. The ESA's consequences will win. Your call, whichever way it goes."

"I'm on it."

Pierce hung up on Miles. He dialed Lindsay's number to check in on her. He shifted about, gearing up for the lies. He couldn't tell her he was so close to home. It wasn't worth blowing his cover.

Lindsay was breathless. "I'm so glad you called. Someone from your company stopped by looking for you. Is everything okay?"

Miles hadn't mentioned the ESA was going to his house.

"All is good. Probably one of my colleagues in town who wanted to catch up."

"It was more like they had news for you or something."

"They'll find me if they do." Pierce's words sent a chill through him.

"How's the audit going?" Lindsay didn't sound convinced.

Pierce made small talk, telling her he loved her, and then hung up. His blood boiled. The Agency was already sending him a warning. He needed to complete his mission and make it home to Lindsay. He needed to protect her. His job may have been a matter of global security, but his heart lived in Lindsay's arms. He had scarcely under a day to get the details to Miles to appease the ESA. Then he could disappear from New Jersey and head back home to his life—and next assignment.

He met Marci at the car. "Where to?"

"DC. We're meeting with Sam Chancellor in about an hour. Think we'll make it with traffic? I heard DC is a nightmare."

"No clue. GPS will help us." Liar. DC was his stomping ground.

The last thing he wanted was Marci talking to a CNN reporter. Before he put the car in drive, he sent a text to Miles.

NEED DC DISTURBANCE. CREATE AN OBSTACLE FOR CNN'S SAM CHANCELLOR.

Miles texted back almost immediately.

CONSIDER IT DONE.

Seconds before they pulled away from Trent's house, a knock on the driver's window startled Pierce. He turned sideways. Trent stood there, his muscles bulging.

"I'm coming."

Marci smiled. Pierce clenched his jaw. He recovered from his blatant annoyance with a relaxed smile. He unlocked the door, letting the oversized state trooper into the car. Nothing about this case was going to be easy. Good thing he had the government on his side in a place where the government ruled most. He forced a sigh of relief.

"Great. Since we're in your neck of the woods, you can navigate."

Marci moved to the backseat. Trent took the passenger's seat. He typed away on his phone as he spoke.

"Head toward the beltway. We have plenty of time. Sam's on his way. He'll wait if we're running late."

Pierce found a local radio station to monitor the effects of Miles's orders. About twenty minutes into the drive, the news reporter interrupted their interview with a top forty band doing a concert at the National Mall for breaking news.

"We've just gotten a report of a car bomber in the middle of DC. Multiple injuries. We aren't sure if there were any fatalities, but we're on top of the story."

Pierce interrupted Marci and Trent's small talk. "Holy shit. A car bomber. Right in the middle of DC."

Marci gasped. "God, no!"

Trent typed frantically on his phone. "Sam's not responding. Let's meet on the outskirts of DC. There's a bar where we can talk. It's obscure. No one will be old enough to know Sam there. Turn here."

Pierce followed suit. He was pleased. He kept up appearances on his concerned demeanor. They wouldn't be meeting Sam. Going to a bar was an excellent alternative. He needed to loosen Trent up to get the real scoop. Marci needed some booze in her, too. A delicate mix. Alcohol to the rescue. The ESA would have their document in no time and be off Pierce's back. A short time later, they found a parking spot and made their way to the bar.

"When will Sam be here?" Pierce asked.

"He never responded. If he was down there, it's mass chaos. Let's get a drink and give him a chance to get here. They have great food, too."

"I'm starving," Marci said.

Trent looked like he was making a call. He put the phone in his pocket and threw his hands up in the air. Pierce pretended not to be watching him. He wasn't entirely because he was scanning the web. He found the post he wanted.

"Oh no," Pierce said with drama. He pulled up short before heading into the restaurant.

"What is it?" Marci looked worried.

Trent stared Pierce down. "Is everything okay?"

Pierce paused before responding. "Your friend Sam. He was one of the ones injured in the car bombing. Explains why he hasn't responded. The report says he's okay. He only sustained minor injuries. It's on CNN's feed."

Trent went on his phone again. "Damn it!"

Pierce put his hand on Trent's shoulder. "Let's get some food. We'll keep up with the reports and get to your friend later."

Marci agreed. "We need to eat. We'll plot plan B."

"Fine."

Trent pushed through the bar's doors. Marci followed. Before Pierce joined them, he sent one last text to Miles.

NICE JOB.

Miles didn't waste any time responding.

WAIT FOR IT.

CHAPTER TWENTY-THREE

AS MARCI EXCUSED herself from the table to hit the bathroom, her phone buzzed. She answered.

"Where are you, honey? It sounds like you're a million miles away." Her mom always called at the worst times.

"I sort of am. I'm in Virginia with a friend. What's up?"

"Ooh, a boy?"

"I'm not a teenager, Ma. We don't call them boys anymore. Yes, it's a guy. Just a friend."

Her mom giggled. "Whatever you say. What's in Virginia?"

"Work. Research. I should be home later. All okay?"

"Oh, yes, everything's fine. I'm just checking in on you." Her voice trailed off in a sad tone.

"You don't sound fine."

She sighed. "I have to apologize for our conversation. We have different beliefs on certain topics. You have more of an open mind than I do. I've always admired that about you. You know I love you no matter what, right?"

"Me too. I'll call you when I get home."

"Be safe, sweetie."

As soon as she hung up with her mom, she called Lou at the hospital. It was the real reason she had left Trent and Peter behind.

"When are they letting you out of that godforsaken place?"

Lou spoke through raspy coughs. "They think it'll be a few weeks between here and rehab. Not soon enough."

Marci closed the door and turned on the water to feign a reason to be in the bathroom. "I'm in Virginia with Trent."

"You don't waste any time." Lou sounded surprised.

"You said I had less than twenty-four hours."

"Much less. Especially for me."

"Did something happen?"

Lou grumbled. "I don't know. I'm probably just paranoid. Especially since I'm so vulnerable here. A man lingered outside my room before you visited. I should have said something, but I let it go."

"What did he look like?"

"From what I could tell, he was tall and thin with dark brown hair, almost black. Dressed like one of those super smart people from the modern sitcoms. Like that Big Bang show, whatever."

"Like a nerd?"

"Smart person, nerd, whatever you want to call him. He had those square glasses, black. It was obvious he was trying to be someone he wasn't. In disguise. He was overdressed for a visit to the hospital. He was lingering right outside of my room and in the doorway like he wanted to come in and talk to me but couldn't pull the plug."

"That's odd. You have no idea who he is?"

"Never saw him before in my life. He had no reason to meet with me unless he was a hospital representative, which may have been the case. Except for what happened after."

A knock at the door startled Marci. She realized she had been in the bathroom way too long. She flushed the toilet to push the process forward.

"Sorry, I have to go in a minute. Tell me what happened."

"He had a short conversation with my nurse, then took off. You came in soon after. Once you headed out, the nurse came into my room. She asked me if I knew who that man was. Apparently he'd asked her a bunch of questions about the hospital's visiting hours and security. She assumed he was an overprotective family member because he seemed concentrated on my room."

"That is a little disturbing."

"To say the least."

Another knock banged at the door. Marci turned off the faucet and unlocked the door. "Call me if anything else happens."

"I will. Tell Trent everything. But only Trent. Make sure it's in private, too. He'll know exactly what to do. Remember, eyes and ears are all over. Corrupt DC folks are swarming like flies around there on the weekend. Don't let that information get into the wrong hands. By the wrong hands, I mean anyone connected with the government. Try to get to the media. That will open up your connections and give you the resources you need to expose them."

"It's in the plan."

Marci slipped the phone into her purse and opened the bathroom door. An older woman with a bad perm and gray roots wobbled in her jean skirt and three-inch heels. A cloud of cigarette smoke and beer breath landed on Marci as the wasted lady pushed her way into the bathroom. The door slammed. Click clacking on the tile floor ensued.

Marci hoped the woman would find the toilet bowl before she passed out.

Back at the table, Peter raised a glass in the air.

"I got you an iced tea. I wasn't sure if you were a day drinker. Alcohol this early in the day isn't for everybody."

Trent was drinking a light beer. A rocks glass with brown liquid sat in front of Peter's paper placemat. She would happily join them in an impromptu early happy hour. Iced tea wasn't enough to quench Marci's thirst anyway.

The server stopped by at the perfect time. "Need a few minutes? It's a standard bar menu if that helps."

"Burger. Well done. Fries. And a whiskey sour."

Trent chugged a quarter of his beer. "Sorry if I was a jerk before. Being a cop changes you. I'm suspicious of everybody."

"Be as jerky as you want. So long as you help us out."

"I'm trying."

"Sorry about your friend Sam."

Marci was the jerk. Trent was trying to help. All she had done was cause him trouble.

"He'll be okay."

"Know anyone else in media?" Peter asked.

"My ex-girlfriend works for *The Entruder*."

Marci's stomach flipped. A smut mag was better than no mag.

"What's her number?"

Peter bristled. "Wait a minute. We drove through four states to get you a tabloid interview?"

Marci winced. Letting Peter come with her was a terrible idea. She should have handled everything herself.

"I'm totally fine with it," Marci said.

"It's cool. I get it. *The Entruder* doesn't have the best reputation. Not exactly on par with CNN." Trent smirked.

"One of my sorority sisters worked for them right out of college. She told me they're a well-run organization. Like TMZ."

"You're in good hands. I promise," Trent said.

The server delivered the food and drinks. "Anything else?"

Peter tapped his glass. "Another round?"

"You got it." The young girl bounced away.

Trent took a bite of his Rueben. "I'll text her. We can meet up today."

"Seems a little awkward." Peter raised his eyebrows in between bites of his cheesesteak.

Trent shrugged. "Nah. We're still in touch. She'll help."

"So long as it's not an issue," Marci said. "Can we meet in about an hour?"

Trent grabbed his phone and sent a text. Two seconds later it buzzed.

"Done. We'll go straight from here."

Peter was looking down at his hands under the table. He was using his phone. Marci wanted to say something. It wasn't her place. When he put it away and looked up, the light glinted on his eyeglass frames. They were the same ones she had noticed on the first day they met. The glasses seemed invisible since then. She forgot he wore them at all. That is until Lou described them perfectly.

A chill spidered through her. She tensed. Marci wanted to sprint out of that restaurant and as far away from Peter as humanly possible.

"Perfect. Let's go," Marci said.

CHAPTER TWENTY-FOUR

PIERCE HAD no information to give Miles except that they were meeting with a reporter from a tabloid magazine. Little did he know, hundreds of people worked for the famous paper, all of which called themselves reporters. For all he knew, Trent's ex-girlfriend was an administrative assistant with no pull whatsoever.

He figured they would meet. He would fill Miles in afterward. Pierce wasn't as concerned with Marci leaking anything to this kind of communications medium. No matter what she said about her experience with the caliber of *The Entruder* staff, their credibility was nothing to worry about. Everyone knew smut magazines published rumors that the public dismissed as garbage. A story of this kind—aliens—might even work in his favor. Marci would look insane versus knowledgeable. Aliens, according to the junk press, had abducted everyone. It probably wasn't the kind of story they would think was sexy enough to take on for publishing. Pierce wasn't worried. Miles was the cautious one. Rightfully so since the last thing they needed was to allow a public slip up.

It was good that Trent was still driving. Pierce didn't want to inadvertently appear to know his way around that area, which, of course, he did. He had lived in that area for the past fifteen years for God's sake.

They pulled down a side street off one of the main roads and headed into a rural area. About five minutes later, Trent was parking on the street lined with row houses. A blonde-haired, trendy woman was waiting for them on the stoop. A pang of embarrassment for Marci's desperation shot through Pierce. Calling Trent eager to please was an under-statement. She stood up, pushing her hair behind her ear and straightening her skirt. The woman hugged her ex-lover hello, noticeably holding onto him a little too long.

"So good to see you, T."

Trent peeled himself away. "Sophie Kincaid, meet Marci Simon. She's the girl I texted you about."

Sophie shook Marci's hand. She looked Pierce up and down.

"And you are?"

"A friend of Marci's."

Pierce leaned in for a handshake. Sophie turned away from him. She opened the door for them to come inside, watching Trent's every move. It was clear Sophie was only interested in helping Marci if it meant getting closer to her ex.

Sophie's row house was more like an upscale brown-stone. Wall-to-wall brick interior. Hardwood floors. Contemporary decor. She had apparently hired a high-end designer. The place looked like a Restoration Hardware magazine layout. For all Pierce knew, it was. After seeing where she lived, he hoped it was no reflection on her level of position at *The Entruder*.

Sophie sat them down at the sprawling farm table that

looked like it was right out of the nineteen hundreds. Lindsay had always wanted a table like that, and even though Pierce could afford it, it didn't fit with their McMansion style home.

Sophie opened her laptop. "Do you mind if I record our session? It's easier than me taking notes. I don't want to miss anything. The law says I need to ask permission. Contrary to popular belief, we do it all by the book at *The Entruder*."

Marci shot Pierce a look. He smiled.

"Where should I start?" Marci asked.

"At the beginning. Of the breaking story, that is."

"Wait," Trent said. "Should we be here? I don't want to jeopardize confidentiality in the story."

He looked away then back at her. He knew something about the business he shouldn't. Sophie's face fell a bit.

"You're absolutely right. I'm so sorry, Marci. I was caught up in the moment. Would you and...what did you say your name was?"

"Peter."

She brushed her hair back behind her shoulder. "Trent, dear, would you and Peter give us a few minutes? Head over to Gus's. I'll text you when we're done."

"Done deal." Trent turned to Pierce. "The bar on the corner."

"That works."

Sophie gave Pierce and Trent a fake smile, waiting for them to leave so she could get down to business with Marci. It was the opposite of what Pierce wanted to happen. He needed to be in the brownstone to hear what was going on. Good thing he came prepared.

He grabbed a little device from his pocket and dropped it behind the couch on the way out. It would record everything within one thousand square feet and livestream it to an audio file on the cloud, which would download onto his phone. A file he could send to Miles within seconds of completion. If it were ever found, it would look like a piece of dirt. The extraterrestrial technology was amazing. Humans had no idea what was out there. If it were up to Pierce, they never would.

CHAPTER TWENTY-FIVE

SOPHIE'S FACE lit up like a Christmas tree.

"Pure gold. We need a multilayer approach to this reveal. We'll start with teasers on social media, ASAP. This would be the perfect content for our pilot series opener, where our top reporters interview key media whistleblowers, called *Now You Know*. Think *TMZ* marries *60 Minutes*."

It was everything Marci wanted. Except she wasn't ready for a camera shoot.

"I'll be on TV?"

"Damn right. This is your big moment. I'll set up hair and makeup. We need to start filming this afternoon."

"No need to go to all that trouble. You can be the one to tell everyone my story. I'll sign whatever you want to give you permission."

Sophie looked at the clock. "Your deadline's almost here."

"That's why I'd rather not be involved."

She sent a text. "Let me get the men back here. We have work to do. I'll need their help." Sophie was ignoring her.

The show would go on with Marci in the spotlight. She didn't want any of it. Disappearances. Deaths. Warnings from Lou and Peter. If Marci went for it, she would live the rest of her life on the run. She didn't want that kind of life. Ever.

"You're the expert. I can't reveal my source anyway. The document says it all. You have everything you need."

Sophie rolled her eyes in more of an annoyed gesture than a condescending one.

"No, honey, you don't understand. The document is the proof. It's our evidence. It's what makes the news credible. Your story, the emotions you'll share are what the public wants. Not some boring document. You, my dear, Marcella Simon, make the story a story at all."

There it was again. The name that had always made her cringe made her feel proud now. She needed a new identity. Her braver personality. She would soon be known to the world as the government whistleblower on the human-alien pact that might cost her life. If she was going to reveal the truth to the public, they might as well know her real name.

"I'll do it."

"Of course you will. Trent and that guy will meet us at headquarters."

Sophie spoke as if she wasn't going to accept anything less from Marci. The media executive grabbed her purse.

Sure enough, as soon as they made their way to the curb, a black limousine was waiting for them. Marci wasn't sure if the driver had superhuman driving skills, ESP, or if it had been planned all along. She did wonder, however, why they couldn't wait another five minutes for Trent and Peter to return so they could all go together. She was confident she would soon find out.

On the drive, Sophie leaned in. "Now tell me, darling. Are you and Trent a thing?"

Marci's mood shifted from a cross between flattery that Sophie would think Trent would be interested and utter denial that any such scenario would be possible.

"Not at all. A good friend connected us."

Sophie raised her eyebrows. "Some good friend."

"Not like that. It's my neighbor. He's Trent's uncle."

After Marci told Sophie about Lou, she crumpled into herself. She had said too much. It wouldn't take long for *The Entruder* to do some investigative reporting and uncover precisely who lived on Cedar Lane who also was related to Trent. The government document would be traced right to General Lou Rollins. In many ways, it made her feel better about coming out on television. At least the focus would be on her, and they would leave poor Lou alone.

"Full disclosure?"

"Go for it."

"Trent and I dated for about six months over a year ago. We've stayed in touch. Although only as friends."

"You still have feelings for him."

"Is it that obvious?" Sophie looked out the window and exhaled.

"It's sweet."

From Marci's viewpoint, Sophie was as vulnerable as they came. She was the kind of woman that would never admit it. It's probably what allowed her to rise to the top of a ruthless industry. She likely easily developed relationships but knew how to change course and be cutthroat when necessary. Sophie straightened and put on a serious face.

"Let's discuss how today will go. Hair and makeup first. Interview prep next. Then the taped interview. I'll be interviewing you, so no surprises. You'll know what I'm going to ask and you'll have a prepared answer. Then we will have the big document reveal. This is where we share the exclusive document in a flash snapshot on television – long enough to see it exists, but not long enough to read it. We'll direct everyone to log on to our website to download the document for a fee. This is huge. Our numbers will go up. Ratings through the roof. You, my dear, will be victorious in your goal to reveal the truth to the world. You'll get a cut of the profits. We'll have a contract ready for you to sign after the episode airs."

Marci thought about it. The money would help. She could fix up Lou's house. Take her leave without stress. Maybe she would even write that novel.

"It's all so overwhelming."

Sophie smiled. "This is a giant step, honey. Be proud of yourself. You're making history."

Marci hadn't thought of it that way. She puffed up a bit. For once in this whole process, the emotion that overcame her wasn't fear or urgency. It was pride.

"I'm ready."

"Good. Because we're here." Sophie winked.

The driver went underground. Marci had missed the view of the outside of the building. After parking in a reserved spot, security escorted them into a private elevator to the penthouse floor where Sophie's office was located.

As managing director of *The Entruder*, Sophie Kincaid was the one in charge. She made the rules. Approved all the stories. Marci was in better hands than she ever imagined. She was oddly thankful she hadn't met with CNN after all. They may have twisted her story and made her look bad. She trusted Sophie because of Trent, and Trent because of

Lou. When they entered Sophie's office, several men were waiting for her.

"We've got the grand arrival," Marci said.

"Always, darling."

The men locked the doors behind Sophie and Marci. Her heart was running a marathon. She had no idea what she would learn. Her gut told her it wasn't anything she wanted to know. Sophie gestured for Marci to sit down at the conference table on the far left of the penthouse, the area designated for work, from what she could tell.

The largest of all the men spoke. "We have new information that you both need to hear. We did a little research. Look what we found."

He slid a file over to Sophie. She opened it. Marci, sitting next to her, read it all. The first page was a photo of Peter and a summary of all his personal and professional statistics. Except the document had to be wrong. Dead wrong. Peter wasn't Peter at all. His real name was Pierce Austin. He was a special agent for the ESA, the elusive and covert government agency dealing in extraterrestrial security.

Sophie turned to Marci. "It's worse than I thought. They're already after you."

Marci shook her head in disbelief. "It must be a mistake."

Sophie closed the file and directed her attention to the man who seemed to oversee the others.

"Find Trent and bring him here. His life is in danger. Hurry!"

CHAPTER TWENTY-SIX

PIERCE EMAILED the audio file from Sophie's house to Miles without having an opportunity to listen to it first and told him so. Pierce had no idea what they discussed. Miles would give him the direction needed to get his job done. Trent hadn't left Pierce's side. He couldn't take a chance on listening to the file in the enemy's presence.

Stopped at a traffic light on the way to meet Marci, Trent's phone buzzed with a text message. His phone's home screen flashed with a note from Sophie.

P IS ARMED & DANGEROUS!

Pierce pretended not to be looking. Timing was perfect because the light turned green and Trent had to drive and didn't pick up his phone. Two traffic lights ahead, black SUVs blocked the roadway.

Thinking quick, Pierce said, "Pull over. I need to use the bathroom."

"Now? Where?" Trent looked around.

Luckily, a coffee shop he knew well was nearby. It had a back door.

"I'll run into the cafe and be right back."

"There's nowhere for me to pull over and wait."

"I'll catch up." Pierce pointed up ahead. "Looks like you'll be sitting for a while."

By the time Trent checked his phone and learned the truth, Pierce would be long gone. As soon as Trent slowed with the traffic, Pierce pushed open the passenger door and walked as quickly as he could without running. He disappeared into the coffee shop. He didn't waste any time. He called Miles as he was weaving his way through the customers and sneaking through the employee door and out the back.

"I need a ride."

"Already on it. Make a right at the corner. Your car is waiting."

Pierce hung up and ran as fast as he could. He jumped into the blacked-out Lexus RX 550. Miles was in the seat next to him. He played the audio file Pierce had sent him. After listening to the recording, Pierce dropped his head in his hands.

"You know what needs to be done," Miles said.

Pierce in no way wanted to kill Marci. He didn't care at all about Sophie, Trent, or anyone else for that matter. Marci was different. Although she was on the wrong side of the fence when it came to acknowledging alien life, he respected her beliefs and passion about the universe. She didn't ridicule it.

"Step one, stop the smut press from revealing the story. Two, secure all forms of the document. Finally, deal with Marci."

Pierce's only redeeming quality was that she was his assignment, and so he had some control.

"I'll handle Marci."

"And by handle, you better mean termination." Miles

was as dangerous as death itself.

"I understand what needs to be done. This isn't my first rodeo either."

Although it was the first rodeo he wanted to lose. Miles raised his eyebrows. He was on to Pierce's soft spot for Marci.

"The alternative. I don't have to tell you."

Lindsay. Pierce shot a look at Miles. "No. You don't."

Pierce dialed the reception desk at *The Entruder*.

"Thank you for calling. We're here for your story. How can I help you?"

"I'm calling to report a suspicious bag left in the elevator. It's headed to the penthouse."

"Sir, we take these calls very seriously. Police will be notified."

"I hope so. It's a bomb. And it's about to detonate." Pierce hung up.

Moments later, Pierce and Miles watched from their SUV a safe two blocks away as windows blew out on the top floor of the paper's main building. Street goers scampered. Alarms went off. Smoke billowed. Within seconds, a rush of people ran out of the building. Minutes later, emergency personnel swarmed the building and news vans showed up.

Mission one, stop the broadcast. Accomplished.

"Bravo, Pierce. You may have accomplished all three missions with that one, brilliant step."

Pierce smiled. A pang sharpened in his chest. He hoped to God he hadn't.

CHAPTER TWENTY-SEVEN

A MOMENT of stillness fell over the penthouse. Marci acknowledged the eerie silence. She didn't have a chance to understand it. An overwhelming blast of sound and a burst of intense illumination engulfed them all. Her senses were on overload for a moment. She flew back against the wall as if someone had shoved her with tremendous force. The physical impact of a sudden jolt of her body nearly knocked her unconscious. She was covered in a thin layer of grit. The sting permeated her skin. Tiny pieces of glass embedded all over her body.

A loud rattling of the giant windows lingered. No. It was more than the windows. The building was trembling. Just like her. The overwhelming sound. The initial confusion of it all. The sense of dread once she realized what had happened. It paralyzed her.

A bomb had gone off.

Was she dead? Marci wasn't sure. She moved her limbs. She was still alive. Pushing her body up to a sitting position, she tried to get her bearings. The room was so dark she could barely see anything. Or hear anything. Sudden and total silence permeated the space. For a moment, Marci feared she had gone deaf. She spoke a few words and couldn't even hear her own voice. Panic set in. Her heart began to race. Okay, so she wasn't blind. She still had her vision. Only her hearing was gone. She had to stop herself from crying and focus on the fact that she was still alive. Maybe the only person alive. She scanned the room. Bodies were strewn about. She was terrified to move. Frozen in utter fear.

What if another bomb exploded? This one didn't kill her. The next one could. How would she escape?

Hyperventilation began. Marci had to calm herself once again. Deep breaths. In and out her nose. Repeatedly. Exactly as she had been taught to do when an anxiety attack set in. Fight or flight. Although appropriate responses, it wasn't a time she could afford to freak out. It was a time she needed to try to survive.

Muffled sounds of car alarms going off startled and relieved her. She wasn't going to be deaf after all. Her hearing was coming back sound by sound. Her ears felt like they were stuffed with cotton. Marci didn't care. Her world wasn't going to be permanently silent. Something she wasn't strong enough to handle. Even if her sense of hearing was damaged, it was better than having no hearing at all.

Marci tried to stand. She staggered to her feet, feeling shakier than she expected. She caught herself before falling over. Seeing clearly wasn't easy. All the air was thick with haze. She wasn't sure if Sophie was in the room with her or in her head. Confused and scared, she stumbled around the space. No one was moving. She called out. Her voice cracked.

"Sophie?"

No answer.

"Where are you?"

No answer.

"Are you okay?"

Still no answer. Marci's heart sank. Sophie must have been dead. Marci was on her own. She prayed she would survive.

"Can anyone hear my voice?"

Silence bellowed louder. Lack of any response frightened her. Maybe they were all passed out. Or worse. Marci moved in the direction of where she thought the elevator doors lived. It was more to get her sense of direction reset rather than to escape. Those doors had opened right onto the penthouse floor. No hallway existed on the top level of the building.

She had neither medical skills to speak of nor any clue on how to survive an emergency like a bomb explosion. All she had going for her was her heart still beating. Being alive was her best asset. Her only option was to leave everyone behind and go get help before she collapsed and became another one of the casualties of the attack. She had been the target all along.

She fingered the inside pocket of her jacket. Everything was still in its place. Thankfully, she had switched to a crossbody bag. That seemed unharmed as well. It was all that mattered. Besides her life, the truth was the most important thing for her to preserve right now.

Her vision getting clearer at times, she could make out an exit sign to her far left. It had to be the stairs. She made her way, tracing her hands along the wall for guidance until she reached the heavy metal door. Sure enough, it was a stairwell.

In the pitch black, she held onto the railing. That was when she remembered she had a keychain flashlight. She sifted through her purse until she pulled it out and pressed the button. It was terribly dim, barely guiding her way down the thirty-something story building.

When she got to the bottom floor, her ears began to ring. She prayed her hearing was coming back to full working order and that this wasn't a sign of her going deaf. She panicked a little again. She was really trying to focus on leaving the building any way possible. She had no idea where she would go from there. Alone, far from home, she had no clue how to reach Trent, and Peter wasn't even Peter anymore. He was her enemy. She wasn't even sure she could trust the police.

Helpless and hopeless, she struggled to push the door open to the lobby. The sweetest sound of Marci's life emanated in the darkness.

"Marci? Are you here?"

He appeared like an apparition coming to life through the thick gray smoke.

"Trent? I'm right here! Help!"

Trent ran to Marci's side. She practically collapsed in her new friend's arms. She wasn't sure if it was from sheer physical, mental, or emotional exhaustion. He lifted her up and carried her out. Her arms around his neck, she had no energy to even thank him. She kept still. Silent. Forever grateful to be alive.

Sirens blared in the streets. Firefighters stormed the building. They burst in after Trent got Marci outside. She didn't have to think of where to go next because the paramedics swarmed her. Trent never left her side. Pedestrians rushed to the explosion site, gawking at the chaos. Police put up temporary barricades to keep the crowd back so they could do their job. All Marci could think of was poor Sophie.

"I don't know if she's okay."

"The EMTs need to take a look at you."

Marci started to cry. "I don't think she made it. I think I'm the only survivor."

Trent's face fell. His words made all the difference.

"Thank God you did."

CHAPTER TWENTY-EIGHT

"LOOKS like you still have your work cut out for you."

Miles pointed to the dramatic scene of Trent carrying Marci out of the building Pierce had just bombed. Pierce's explosion hadn't killed her. His heart fell in confused relief. He feigned disappointment in his expression to Miles.

"You have got to be kidding me."

"We'll get that document one way or another."

Pierce cringed inside. He was proud of Marci. She was a survivor. A believer. He had all the faith in the world she would make it. He had to prove to the ESA that he was serious. To save her life, Pierce would have to turn her mindset around somehow. Only he wasn't about to share that with Miles the Murderer, as he was dubbed at the Agency. Pierce had to play the ESA's game.

"For Christ's sake, if blowing up a building didn't kill her..."

"Don't ask what can kill her, because you know I have thousands of ways on my mind. And thousands more ways yet to be dreamed up."

Pierce's stomach twisted and churned. "We'll try them all."

"I say we torture the truth out of her. Then you can kill her with your bare hands."

"Can't wait."

Miles yelled to the driver. "Pull over. We'll walk from here. I'll signal you when we need another pickup."

He opened the door to the SUV. Pierce followed suit.

"She's signing a release so they won't take her in the ambulance."

"A little foot action. We'll hunt them down the old-fashioned way."

Because of Sophie, Marci now knew Pierce's true identity. His cover was blown. All bets were off. Pierce's only mission was to stop Marci at any cost. He would do his job, primarily while he was on Miles's watch. Pierce didn't have his same old drive any longer. His change of heart was quite disturbing. There had to be another way for all of this to end. A better way than for Marci to die. For now, he needed to follow the ESA's rules. He would figure out an alternate ending to this story when the time came.

"They're on the move. Let's go." Miles slipped on his black shades and secured his hand at his waist where his weapon was loaded and ready for firing.

Pierce mimicked his motions, keeping a safe distance behind them.

"Let's hang back a bit. He sees us."

"They're ESA fugitives. We can't hang back."

Miles picked up his pace. Pierce jogged alongside him. Trent apparently knew his way around the city, weaving in and out of the crowd. He was also smart enough to realize he and Marci were being followed. Trent's over-the-shoulder glance every block confirmed Pierce's suspicions.

He spotted a crowd of about a hundred people up ahead. Protestors were a common sight in the capital. Yet today wasn't the day for additional obstacles.

"We need to gain on them. We can't lose them in the mayhem."

"I'm on it."

Miles began to run. Trent sensed the shift in the cat and mouse game because without looking back, he locked arms with Marci. He practically dragged her into the center of the sea of protestors.

"Damn it."

Pierce wasn't sure if he meant it or if he was caught up in the moment as well. He tried to focus on his goal. Allowing his emotions to interfere with what needed to be done meant the death of everything.

"We're going to separate once we get into the crowd. Your goal is Marci. Mine is Trent. I don't care if we have to pull their arms off to get them into custody. We're not leaving without them." Miles's jaw clenched.

"I'm on it."

Pierce couldn't see where they went to save his life. He split off from his partner anyway. Miles darted to the left through the crowd. Pierce went to the right. One of them would catch up with the couple. Then they would have to follow Agency orders only. Pierce knew precisely what that meant. He had to separate Marci from Trent, even if only to save her life for a few more hours.

Pierce pushed through the crowd, false starts happening every few feet. It was a sea of people. They all looked like Marci and Trent. He wondered if he would ever find them. And then he got lucky.

Marci turned around. She caught Pierce's gaze. A familiar expression of knowing flashed over her face before terror took hold. She nudged Trent. He dragged her down an alleyway. Pierce wasn't sure if Miles had seen them. This was his only chance.

He raced after them. Right before they got away, he pulled the weapon from the left side of his belt and fired. Pierce hit Trent. He fell hard, releasing Marci. Trent was slumped by a dumpster, where he would lie until Miles retrieved him. He refrained from shooting her. She had been through enough. He sprayed her with a fast-acting, mild sedative that would subdue her for only ten or fifteen minutes. Pierce caught her as she fell. He carried her a few blocks away. He messaged Miles to let him know he had Marci secured. Pierce told Miles where Trent was lying on the ground in the place he had hit him with a tranquilizer dart.

"Take him in for questioning," Pierce said via talk to text to his partner. "I'll meet you at the Agency's satellite office within the hour."

Miles texted him.

GOOD WORK.

All of Pierce's tension released. When he looked down at Marci, his chest tightened again. An innocent woman trying to do what she believed was the right thing. He could relate to her on so many levels. He wished the situation didn't have to come to life or death. It was how everything always turned out. For civilians like Marci, the Agency always got what they wanted.

Miles, a senior special agent, rarely passed on a compliment to anyone, let alone Pierce. Even though on the same team, Miles was always in competition with Pierce. He supposed the reason his partner was readily dishing out praise now was so he could get exactly what he wanted later if strings needed to be pulled. Reciprocation theory. When one person did something for another, even in the form of a compliment, they would feel obligated to reciprocate. Pierce wanted praise, so Miles gave it. He would expect Pierce to give him what he wanted next time.

Pierce focused on Marci. He tried not to analyze what his extended future might look like. Dealing with the next hour or two was all he could handle. He needed a plan. When Marci awoke, he would tell her everything. And pray she would understand. He could really use someone like her on his side. The only way to get her there would be full disclosure.

Marci's eyes began to open. "Peter. No—Pierce. What the hell are you doing?"

"Saving your life."

"Trent already did that. You're trying to kill me."

"That's my job. You're going to help me fail."

"You've lost your mind."

"Maybe. But my partner Miles is crazier than me. He'll kill Trent if we don't stop him."

Tears welled in Marci's eyes. "I won't let that happen. Lou can't lose another person he loves. I'm the one that started the trouble. I'll take the heat."

Pierce understood her concern. Protecting Lou or Trent wasn't an option. If Pierce was going to protect anyone, it was going to be Marci.

"Whether you believe me or not, and right now I don't blame you if you don't, I don't want to harm you. Miles and the Agency aren't on the same page with me. I can protect you, but you need to trust me."

"Why would I trust you? You've lied to me from day one."

"I'm not lying to you now. Your life is in serious danger. I can save you."

"Save Trent. That's what I want."

Pierce absorbed the wrecked image of Marci standing before him. A pang flashed through his heart. He had caused her immense pain. Bloody wounds were his doing. Worse, the emotional and psychological damage were also his handwork. She had survived the bomb explosion. He may have damaged her in ways only the future would reveal. Maybe he changed her for the worse. Killed her fighting spirit. She was already dead. He was to blame.

"I'll need your cooperation."

"Shoot."

"Hand over that classified document, for starters. It'll postpone any undue harm from the Agency. Then you need to retract your post on *Among Us*. As well as your stance on extraterrestrial experiences, encounters, beliefs, and so forth. Publicly."

"You really want my soul?"

"I really want you to work for us."

Unbridled fury raged in Marci's eyes. "I'd rather die."

"Your wish may very well come true."

CHAPTER TWENTY-NINE

MARCI STARED out the taxi's window with her back to Pierce. The stubborn silence was her weapon. At least he had spared her the torture of riding in an Agency car. She was grateful for his spit of mercy. She would never let him know. She scanned the streets as they weaved through the city looking for anyone that resembled Trent. Until she had proof he was safe, she wasn't going to give Pierce anything—information or otherwise.

They pulled up to an unassuming and partly dilapidated brick building off the main road. Marci exited the cab and followed quietly behind Pierce. He led her through an unmarked metal door. A private location for a formal top-secret meeting. Marci felt like she was preparing to greet a gang of mobsters instead of an established, albeit underground, government agency. A musty basement smell permeated the air. A layer of dust covered everything. Not the kind of place used for gatherings on a regular basis. The Agency apparently didn't care what its visitors thought of the space. It was practically a garbage dump. Pierce gestured to a beat-up metal table surrounded by a few folding chairs.

"Have a seat."

"Interrogation time."

Marci's body tensed. She wanted to kick something or someone across the room. Break something. Punch her fury out. What was the point of surviving if she would be treated like a hardened criminal anyway? She had no idea where Trent was. If he was alive or dead. Maybe she would never see him again. Heat rushed her. Why did she care about him at all? Because Lou cared. The last thing she needed was to tell him she got his only living relative killed.

"More like psychological torture."

Pierce paced around the room. It was as if he was waiting for another person to arrive. Marci wasn't restrained in any way. She wasn't sure why not. Nothing was stopping her from jumping up and dashing out of that horrific place. Being small and light worked in her favor. She was fast. Pulling her phone out was another option. Why not just call the police? Unless Pierce already knew none of it would help her. He would catch her. Sedate her. Maybe even kill her. Alternatively, they could have guards outside the door. On the street. All over DC. The police were probably in on it, too. Of course they were. It was the government.

Her posture sagged. No need to be restrained. No escape was possible. Being held captive, whether in that room or in life, frightened her to the core.

"When do we start?"

"In about five minutes. You'll have a chance to decide on your fate. Choose wisely."

"I already told you my decision. Save Trent. Not me."

Her words betrayed her. She was nowhere near as brave as she sounded. She didn't want to die. It was the last thing she wanted. She didn't know why she was risking her life for a stranger she had just met. For all she knew, Trent was the biggest jackass on the planet. Marci had just given up her last breath to save his life. Pierce came close to her.

"Trent may be a bargaining chip. He's not worth that much. Miles will have no mercy. He'll be furious it's gotten to this stage. My job is to convince him to spare your life. I'm your only salvation. I can't do it alone."

"You tried to kill me. Now you've kidnapped me. Salvation, my ass."

"True. In my defense, I'm just doing my job."

"You suck at it."

"Truer yet."

"Take it to the next level. Fail with honors. Let me go."

"No can do."

"You say you want to save me. Yet you're keeping me here until Miles gets ahold of me. Sick bastard."

"You're my assignment, yes. But I have feelings, too. I have a family—a wife at home. I know what good people look like. Not only good people. People the world needs. You're one of them."

Marci's heart softened a bit. She wanted to believe him for so many reasons. It wasn't smart. Enamored by his words or not, she needed to protect herself.

"Then let me go."

"I can't do that. I can't go against Agency orders. I can only work out a deal at this point. If you don't help me, the consequences I warned you about will come to fruition on Miles's terms: without mercy."

Marci didn't have a chance to respond before the door burst open. Miles had Trent tied in chains like an animal. His mouth was stuffed with a rag and taped shut so tightly around his head that he couldn't move his neck. She could tell it was hard for him to breathe because he was sweating profusely. Mucus streamed out of his nose that he kept clearing to get oxygen in. It was disgusting treatment of a human being. It showed Marci precisely what she believed all along. The government looked at civilians like they were rabid dogs on a chain. No love for humanity. No love lost in abusing people. So long as their agenda was being pushed, they all slept like babies every night.

Miles tossed Trent in the corner of the room like a piece of meat. Her new friend scrambled to a sitting position. He couldn't stand on his own. Marci rose to help him. Miles pushed her down with brute force. Pierce's expression told Marci he wasn't pleased. He bit his lip and allowed it anyway. Miles towered over Marci, intimidating her with his demeanor of power.

"Where do you think you're going?"

"You can't do that to him. He's a human being. What's the matter with you people?"

Miles raised his eyebrows. "Gee, I don't know. We're sadistic bastards. Maybe, just maybe, we're trying to protect little peons like you from a world you don't understand. And never will."

"We can't understand what we don't know. You won't tell us the truth. That's exactly what I'm trying to do. Maybe if people knew the reality, they would stand up against the enemy. Which shouldn't be our own government."

"You have absolutely no idea what you're talking about. Shut your mouth," Miles said.

"It's in your best interest to do as we say, little miss blogger," Pierce said.

"We want that document, at a minimum." Miles was spitting in Marci's face with his words.

"I'm not selling my soul to Satan. Sorry, fellas."

"No soul selling here. Just survival."

"It's overrated."

"You don't want anything to happen to your new friend over there, do you?"

After Miles spoke, as if on cue, two oversized goons entered the room. They barreled toward Trent. One lifted him off the ground, while the other punched him about ten times. Trent grunted and moaned, twisting in pain. He had nowhere to go. He had to take the abuse. Marci screamed for them to stop. No one listened.

"No more."

Pierce pointed at the men. "Listen to the woman."

They did. The huge men let go, and Trent fell hard on the concrete floor. He writhed in pain. Marci couldn't take it anymore. She stood up and turned to help Trent. Miles grabbed her shoulder and slammed her into the chair.

"Don't make us restrain you, Ms. Simon."

Marci spoke through gritted teeth. "Then leave Trent alone."

"Are you reconsidering?" Pierce asked.

Marci looked over her shoulder at Trent. He shook his head at her. He didn't want her to give anything up to them. No matter what they did to him. Marci was conflicted. Information was power, something she wasn't used to having. She was in control and ready to use it to Trent's advantage. Whether he wanted her to or not.

"Take the duct tape off his mouth. He's hardly breathing."

"In exchange, you will do what?" Miles asked.

Marci racked her brain for an in-between offering.

"I'll tell you how to retrieve the details I gave the paper

so the story doesn't get out. We all know your bomb didn't stop that process."

"It's a start."

Miles nodded at one of the men. One of the massive men ripped the tape off Trent's mouth. He spit the rag out of his mouth, gasping between coughs.

"Don't tell them anything."

Another goon kicked Trent. "Shut your mouth."

Marci put her hand up. "It's okay."

Pierce called the attackmen off Trent, while Miles pulled out a chair next to Marci.

"What don't we know?"

"You hack into computer systems, don't you?"

Miles rolled his eyes. "Clearly. Why?"

"When Sophie and I were discussing the details for the broadcast reveal, she uploaded the information I shared to a secure cloud online. She told me no matter what happened to the tabloid's files, the cloud documentation would be backed up permanently with triple layers of protection."

"We took down their computer systems and backup storage off-site. We checked the cloud and deleted all the files."

Marci shook her head. "The cloud they have visible is a cover. They store the real files in an online server that only Sophie can access. It belongs to her personally."

"You know this, how?"

"For one, she told me."

"For two?"

"I watched her log in. I even noted her username and password."

"Well, well, well, Ms. Simon. It looks like we have an amateur hacker on our hands." Miles laughed with a devious tone.

Pierce smirked. "Marci's full of useful surprises."

Maybe he had a point about her value to the ESA beyond Lou's document. The advantage of her worth would be her greatest asset. Miles nodded to one of his minions. His minion went to the other side of the room, opening an attaché case on a small table. He pulled out a laptop and brought it over to Miles. He opened it, and then tapped a few keys to log online.

"Log into the cloud. Everything you do on this machine is recorded so there's no need for you to dictate what you're doing. Just get me access to Sophie's personal files."

He slid the laptop over to Marci. Marci's fingers trembled as she typed in the address for Sophie's personal cover website, the same place where she sold her bestselling book, *Living a Tabloid Life*. The media executive's bright smile was plastered on her site header, the light in her ocean-blue eyes unmistakable and full of life. A pang of pain hit Marci's heart. She had been the reason Sophie was killed. Marci's selfish desire to reveal a truth she wasn't even sure was hers to tell, had not only murdered Sophie and her staff. It also put Trent's life in danger, and who knew what else was to come. None of it would be good. It was too late. The damage had been done. Turning back now wasn't an option.

Marci took in a deep breath. She clicked on Sophie's camera-up-in-flames logo. It took Marci to a page where she could log in. Although it looked like she would get information on her media kit and private groups, a tiny icon of *The Entruder* appeared. When she clicked on it, it took her to a back-office site. If anyone else clicked on it, it would look like a black screen. Marci watched as she double-clicked and a box popped up for a username. Her photographic memory came in handy now. She entered: SuperSophie07.

It prompted Marci for the password, which she couldn't help but remember: TrentRollins15.

Marci nodded. Miles's eyes grew wide. He licked his lips. He snatched the laptop from Marci.

"We're in."

"Pure gold."

Pierce leaned over Miles to watch his every move. Marci hung her head. She immediately regretted her decision.

CHAPTER THIRTY

PIERCE JOINED Miles at the computer. Marci's face changed from relief to regret. She had done precisely what they asked. He hoped Miles and the Agency would merely erase her memory and set her free.

"You did the right thing, Marci."

Miles was scanning it all, undoubtedly searching for the government document that turned all eyes to Marci to begin with. Marci faced Trent. Her expression was covered in guilt and pain.

"Now you can let Trent go."

Pierce nodded. Miles gave him a nasty look.

"Unchain him and bring him here," Pierce said.

"He's your problem if he makes any moves," Miles said.

"I'm pretty sure Thing 1 and Thing 2 can handle Trent."

Pierce tapped Miles's shoulder in reassurance. Marci had done an honorable deed. One that was beyond what most would do for a stranger they just met. She gave up her beliefs and handed the key to it all to a person who was as corrupt as they came.

"Yes. Here we go."

Miles smiled wide, seeming to find what he was looking for. He opened the document until it filled the computer screen. Marci looked down, an expression of disappointment and failure on her face. Pierce wanted to comfort her. It wasn't appropriate. Thing 1 shoved Trent into the seat next to Marci. Pierce watched as Marci tried to calm Trent, mouthing not to do anything stupid.

Pierce examined the evidence. He confirmed it was a scanned version of the missing document from 1968 when Lou encountered the UFO. All those involved in that incident had since passed from documented natural causes.

"The last piece of proof," Miles said with a smirk.

"Excellent," Pierce said.

"Problem is, we still don't have the original."

"This is what you asked for. I handed it to you on a 'pure gold' platter just like you said," Marci said.

"Not entirely. You're too young to know this, but you're a smart girl, so let me re-educate you. Back in the sixties, there were no computers. It was all paper. That's it. If Sophie loaded this document online, she must have had a paper copy to scan first."

Marci paused for a moment as if considering her answer. "I gave Sophie the document electronically. The original has been destroyed."

Pierce wanted to believe her. He and Miles had been trained extensively in how to spot a liar. Marci looked down and to the left before she responded. A subtle yet indicative mark of someone not telling the truth. Miles was about to unleash a rage that would terrify even Pierce. He tried to get ahead of the deadly situation.

"Do you take me for a complete idiot?" Miles asked.

Trent jumped in. "Relax. She said it was destroyed. It was destroyed. You have what you want. Now let us go."

Miles began to laugh, a sadistic laugh as if he was going to find so much joy in torturing them he could hardly stand it.

"Another brainiac."

"Your insults suit your personality," Marci said.

Pierce was becoming increasingly concerned for Marci's safety. She was pushing Miles to a new breaking point. His partner shoved the laptop aside and leaped to his feet. Pierce was close enough to Miles to prove his loyalty, but in a sideways position where he could block him from attacking Marci if need be. Miles hovered over his two prisoners.

"Do you know what we could do to you right now if we wanted to? You're messing with global security. Your right-eousness is putting the world at risk."

"If the claims of UFO sightings, alien abductions, and government conspiracies are hoaxes, then why are we at risk?"

"We didn't mention a hoax," Miles said.

"You're confirming it's all true," Marci said.

"We didn't confirm a thing," Pierce said.

"Not fake. Not real. Make up your minds. Which is it?" Marci asked.

"Neither," Miles said.

"I give up," Marci said.

"Civilians aren't privy to our information. Classified information in the hands of someone who doesn't under-stand its power can be deadly. True power is a dangerous thing. Sharing it with a tabloid or the public at large puts humanity at risk for more reasons than you can fathom.

We're doing this, believe it or not, for not only your own good but for the sake of all mankind," Pierce said.

Marci rolled her eyes. "That's a story for *The Entruder*. Maybe the big screen. It's an award-winning performance. Save it for them. I want the truth. And I want everyone alive to know it."

"That's never going to happen, with or without that document. Your life means nothing to us. If we can save millions, we'll be happy to sacrifice who we need to," Miles said.

"Clearly. You've been doing it for decades."

"We don't have the stupid piece of paper you're looking for. You have the damn files. We're done here." Trent stood. Thing 2 shoved him back down into the chair.

"Not quite done. This little lady has one last opportunity to tell us where that document is or she'll be terminated, alongside you."

"I'll be the one to do it. Don't make me, Marci," Pierce said.

Pierce wanted to object. He had no choice. Acting calm and cool was the only option. Taking control was his only control. He needed to publicly get Miles out of it because Miles would terminate anyone for any reason or no reason at all, with his eyes closed and a latte in one hand.

"I told you. I destroyed it. I knew how dangerous it was —Lou warned me. All that's left is the electronic file."

Pierce looked at the download. An error message appeared. They needed that document. He didn't want to egg Miles on anymore. Pierce discreetly tried to re-download it, but the file shut down and the cloud account disappeared. Pierce decided to play it cool—he summoned Thing 1 to shut down the computer.

"We have the e-file. We've taken one step in the right

direction. We still need the piece of paper," Pierce said. "You know its worth. You never would have destroyed it."

"I did."

Miles stood and brushed off his shoulders.

"We'll just have to find the document ourselves. In the meantime, Pierce is in charge."

He summoned the two goons to leave with him. Pierce exhaled a small breath of relief only he could hear.

"I expect when I return in the hour, we'll have two dead bodies to dispose of. Yes?" Miles asked.

Marci and Trent looked at each other. Pierce didn't give them any reassurance. He stayed in character with Miles.

"Consider it done."

CHAPTER THIRTY-ONE

THE DOOR SLAMMED behind Miles and his two goons. Chains rattled and clanged. Marci's heart dropped at the muscular man being treated like a convict. The Agency's hideaway was more like a medieval prison than a meeting space. She couldn't believe her own government condoned such treatment of those who served them. It disgusted her to the core.

Trent leaped to his feet. He rushed Pierce sideways, nearly knocking him to the ground. The agent maintained his footing somehow. Pierce snapped back into Trent. For a slender man, Pierce was strong. He wasn't as visually muscular as Trent, but powerful nonetheless. Pierce stopped him in his tracks. Words flew from Trent's mouth like shrapnel, loud and coarse through his gritted teeth.

"This is bullshit. Let us go."

"No can do."

He slid a device from his right jacket pocket and pressed it to Trent's temple. It wasn't a gun or a Taser. It was something she had never seen before. From where she sat, it looked like a portable charger: a thick, round metal device.

"Death is an option."

"Peter, Pierce, whatever your name is...stop." Desperation filled her tone. "Take me. Leave Trent out of it."

"Don't listen to her. She's worth saving. If you need to pull the trigger on someone to show your partner you mean business, do me."

Marci flew up from her chair and pushed between the two men.

"I'm not joking, Pierce. They want me. It's me they'll get."

Pierce penetrated her gaze, a hint of anger behind his eyes, but more so pride. He dropped the device from Trent's temple. Pierce dragged him back to his seat. Trent raged against the metal chains. Pierce grabbed Marci by the arm more gently than she anticipated. He walked her to her seat as well. He straightened his posture.

"Let's be civilized, shall we? We'll get more accomplished that way."

"Civilized treatment would be removing Trent's chains."

"Get this shit off me. You can't expect me to cooperate and behave like a human being when you treat me like a wild animal."

"He's right. Take off his restraints, and we'll cooperate. Or you can kill us like your partner wants."

"For someone who doesn't want to be treated like an animal, you're certainly acting like one who needs to be sedated."

Pierce reached into the inside of his jacket and pulled out a syringe. Marci went into pure survival mode.

"Unlock Trent. I'll handle the syringe. I baste turkeys for Thanksgiving. It can't be much different."

She took the device from his hands. He let her. Shaking, she turned around. With her back to Pierce, she pressed on the syringe alongside Trent's arm. He slowly relaxed, almost into a sleep state. His eyes were still open. Marci slipped the needle into her pocket.

"Trust 101. Did I pass?" Marci smirked.

"You're on your way."

Pierce unlocked Trent's chains and threw them to the side of the room. Trent didn't move an inch. Marci was on her best behavior as well. They had a plan. Even though they had never discussed it.

"Now that we're civil and cooperative, where is the original document?"

"In New Jersey," Marci said.

"Where?"

"I'll show you when we get there."

Pierce's face tightened. "Not good enough."

"It has to be."

He slammed his fist on the table. "Where is it?"

Marci shook slightly. She prayed she could pull it off. "Locked up. In a safe. At home."

Pierce's shoulders fell in relief. Her explanation made sense.

"You didn't destroy it, as I suspected."

"I didn't trust Miles. But for some crazy reason, I trust you."

Marci half meant it, too. Pierce's face softened. Her attempt to connect with him had worked. Even if he had been assigned to her from the get-go, they had shared a few moments of understanding, even if over their love for the night sky. It was her time to exploit it to the fullest.

Pierce took out his phone and pressed a button to record.

"What's the combination? I'll need specific instructions as to where it's located so my men can retrieve it immediately. It's the only way to save your life at this point. Accuracy is of utmost importance."

"Neither."

Pierce looked confused. "Some digital unlock button, then?"

"Like I said, we need to go back to New Jersey."

"We can't go back to New Jersey, at least not with you."

"You'll have to. My safe only opens with my fingerprint."

"We'll need to ensure your fingerprint is transported safely to New Jersey."

Pierce pulled out what looked like a metal pen. Trent's eyes watched Pierce's every move. He pointed the pen at an empty chair. After pressing a button on the top of it, the farthest-tool-from-a-pen severed a metal leg off with surgical precision.

"I'm sorry, Marci. I never wanted to hurt you. But it's come down to a loss of one of your extremities to save your life. It's worth it, no?"

Marci's heart pounded in time with the migraine forming. Was he really going to sever her finger right there in that disgustingly dirty room?

"Don't do this. Take me to New Jersey. I'll get you the document."

"I can't do that. This is the only option."

"You'll have my fingerprint. You won't have the location of my safe."

"We'll find it. I'm not worried."

Trent was limp and quiet as if he were sedated and unable to move.

"You won't. It's not in the house. You'll need me to locate the safe."

Pierce seemed to consider her words for a moment. He grabbed her right hand and pressed it flat on the table.

"We have what we need. Are you going to tell me what finger, or should I just lop off both of your hands?"

"Please don't do this."

"Fine. I'll start with your dominant hand."

Marci closed her eyes and screamed.

CHAPTER THIRTY-TWO

PIERCE BACKED himself into a corner this time. He had no choice. Severe and forceful action was required. The very last thing he wanted to do was to hurt Marci, especially not turn her into an amputee, or worse, take her life. His options weren't pretty.

He pointed the laser at her hand until a thin blue line appeared on her wrist. It would sever her hand in its entirety while cauterizing it at the same time. Extraterrestrial technology at its best. Although initially meant for the medical field and not for harm, such a device had many purposes.

Sweat was beading up on Marci's brow. Her eyes were filled with tears. Pierce's heart broke a little as he recognized a brief glimpse of Lindsay in Marci's expression. Fragility didn't discriminate. A woman in desperate need of love wasn't hard to find. Pierce wished he could comfort her. Tell her everything was going to be all right. That would be a lie. Even a lie would be better than the truth right now. Lies were often better, as he had learned in his work over the years. Ignorance was pure bliss, especially when it came to the truth about the universe. Knowing what was out there was the true meaning of death.

He took a deep breath, reconciling what needed to be done. Right when Pierce was about to push the button, doing the unthinkable for the sake of humanity, Marci's scream penetrated every cell in his body. He hesitated. It was barely enough time for Trent to spring up from his chair. He pounced on Pierce, slamming him to the ground. Pierce struggled to reach any one of his minuscule weapons. Marci was wrapping the chains around his wrists and feet like a professional. Had she done this before? He didn't care. It was clear Pierce needed her on his side of the war zone, and now.

"We gave you an out. You blew it."

Marci breathed heavy, struggling against the robust chains. She hooked the locks in place, too tight for Pierce. He refused to complain. He had been through worse.

"We trusted you. I let you in my house."

Trent punched Pierce in the jaw with a force he didn't know still existed in men. The energy behind Trent's fist was pure loathing. Blood pooled in Pierce's mouth. He spit it out to the side as best he could lying on the concrete floor.

"You've made a terrible mistake."

He couldn't save them now. Marci's hand was worth her life. When Miles got ahold of them, he would sever both her hands. Then he would revel in splattering the rest of her and Trent all over the streets of DC in the midday sunlight right before erasing everyone's memory in the vicinity. He would find the document anyway. Ignorance was bliss. It could also exterminate humans.

"Looks like you're the one suffering for it," Marci said.

Marci's twisted features told Pierce she was furious. The tide had turned all the way around. She would have killed him if she could have. Her eyes steamed with violence. When they finished securing the chains, they dragged him to the corner of the room near an exposed pipe. Trent grabbed the chain tightened over his wrists. He wrapped it around the tube and secured it with the third and final lock. Pierce wasn't going anywhere unless rescued. Trent put the key in his pocket. He ransacked Pierce's jacket.

"What is all this stuff?" Trent asked.

"I wouldn't attempt to use any of it. You'll kill yourself."

"Throw it all in here. We'll test it out later," Marci said.

She opened her purse. Trent dumped everything he found—from the laser to the pen to other odd devices they had never seen before—into her bag.

"Your bag is a bomb, Marci."

"I've survived bombs."

Marci's face grew pale. She was in uncharted territory. Pierce couldn't help her; all he could do was pray for a good outcome for the Agency, and Marci.

"I already met the devil, and I chained him up and left him for dead. I'm good. Thanks for the warning."

Pierce scooted up to a more comfortable position. "Suit yourself. I could have done something. Now it's too late."

Trent kicked Pierce. "Stop it with the melodrama. You're no different than your friend over there that wanted us dead. Don't act like you were on our side. You double-crossed Marci and were willing to cut off her hand to get what you wanted. You're a piece of shit in a three-piece suit."

"We should get going. I'm sure our other 'man in black' isn't far behind."

"Good call."

"Wait," Marci yelled. "One last thing."

Trent stopped in his tracks and turned around. Marci leaned down to Pierce and whispered.

"This is for not killing me."

She pulled out the full syringe she had taken from Pierce when she feigned sticking Trent. She shoved it into Pierce's arm and pressed the piston.

CHAPTER THIRTY-THREE

LOU SHIMMIED himself up in his hospital bed. No longer using a conventional springboard mattress, the cheap hospital used plastic-wrapped airbeds. They were for shit. With every move, a motor buzzed loudly trying to compensate for the weight. The piece of crap bed kept Lou up all night. When he wasn't trying to sleep, his back was gnarled into a thousand knots. New layers of arthritis had formed. He was sure of it. The nurse came in with his medication at dawn, as usual.

"Here you go. You've got your vitamin B, aspirin, and your heart meds. The usual."

"Alrighty."

Lou took a sip of water. He dumped the cup of pills into his mouth and swallowed.

"Breakfast is right behind me."

"Thanks, uh..."

He couldn't remember the woman's name for the life of him. Sure enough, the cafeteria girl waltzed in the room. Lou made room on his tray for all the food. He took the top off. It was smelly. Watery scrambled eggs, a piece of dry toast, and some fruit stared back at him. He supposed it would be good enough. Coffee would save him, even though it was weak and lukewarm.

The only redeeming feature in that place was that he was staying a private room. No roommate to speak of, which was a gift. Lou had suppressed his social skills for years now, revealing himself only to Marci and his long-lost nephew, Trent.

He took a few bites of the breakfast when he noticed a shadow in the hallway, which was otherwise quiet. Lou had a brief surge of anxiety. He went back to eating his terrible meal, distracting himself. Random people were wandering the hospital floor always. He often wondered about hospital security. He resolved himself to the fact that none existed. Doctors and nurses were too busy to pay attention to the buzzers the patients pushed, let alone a stranger entering a patient's room that didn't belong. They would never know.

Something dark stirred inside of Lou's gut. He dropped his fork. He had a bad feeling. Lou's bad feelings could be trusted. They were from years of government training and exposure to things no sane person ever wanted to see. They always meant terrible things were about to happen.

He put the lid on his food and decided to pay attention. The curtain around his bed was open, so only half of the doorway was exposed. The doctor had forgotten to pull it all the way back the last time he examined him. Lou hadn't summoned the energy to get up and move it himself or make a point to ask the nurse. Instead, he pressed the button to move his bed until he was in an upright position, shifting under the air pockets to get comfortable. He peeked his head around the curtain and jumped back a bit.

A tall man, all dressed in black, stood before him. Lou knew precisely where he was from before a word was said.

He wore dark glasses, even inside the hospital. While security wasn't excellent, Lou would have expected someone to question him. Those men had the ability, whether through persuasion or technology, to get what they wanted.

Lou sat back and intertwined his fingers to calm down and pray. He knew what was coming. He would never escape it.

"General Rollins."

The man's demeanor was deep, dark, and emotionless. Lou took an audible breath. He refused to respond. The man shook his head.

"Trent was a naughty nephew. Your neighbor Marci didn't cooperate with us either. We tried to work with you. Years ago, we trusted you. We were wrong to do so. We know that now, albeit too late."

The man made his way to the side of Lou's bed. Lou swallowed hard. Lou made his peace with what was about to happen, even though he wasn't sure how. He prayed it wouldn't hurt. More so, he prayed for Trent and Marci.

"Take me. Spare them."

Lou's plea was desperate. The man in black, the ESA agent, laughed aloud.

"Not an option."

"You'll never find the document. If you kill them, you'll never get what you're looking for. The truth will be revealed to the world no matter what you do."

The ESA agent tilted his head. "You know us better than that, General Rollins. You used to believe that was the right thing to do. What changed? You disappointed us."

"You took my family. No going back from that."

The agent scratched his chin. "It happens."

Lou straightened and began to recite the Hail Mary. The agent broke off a piece of toast and examined it. Slowly he pried open Lou's lips. The man in black shoved the toast into Lou's mouth, covering it with his hand so no sound could come out. He tilted Lou's head back and squeezed his throat.

Lou was choking. A natural death. At least they would give who was left in his family that much dignity. Possibly, for his service to the Agency all those years ago. Or maybe to cover it all up. Either way, Lou was somewhat grateful.

The oxygen in his lungs was evaporating. His body struggled against his will to die. Survival mode took over. Lou fought against it. His time had come. No use in fighting to live. The outcome would be the same. No reason to struggle until the bitter end of his life. The man's hands clenched increasingly. His face never showed any emotion. Lou didn't take it personally. It was the man's job. He understood.

Lou drifted off into altered consciousness. The dream-like state paraded him through the most important moment from his life on Earth. Gratitude filled him to almost bursting. Irene and Eric appeared before him. He reached his hand out to touch them. He couldn't wait to be with them again for eternity. Love replaced any lingering fear. His heart and soul were complete.

Lou slipped into the other side. His world went dark forever.

CHAPTER THIRTY-FOUR

TRENT GRABBED MARCI'S ARM. They bolted out of the makeshift prison they had been trapped in for the last hour. When they got to the street, Trent looked both ways. He ran with purpose to the right. After a half of a block, he turned left down a small alleyway. Marci was on his tail.

"Where we headed?"

"To find a car."

"Your car's nowhere near here."

"I didn't say *my* car."

Marci didn't bother to ask. Her only goal was to try to keep pace with Trent. The man apparently knew how to weave his way around the convoluted city. Trent stopped short. He eyed a limousine as the driver made his way to the building to get the packages from his client.

"Follow me."

"Where else would I go?"

Marci didn't even try to resist. Trent flew to the driver's side door and jumped in. Marci got in the passenger's seat. Within seconds, they were far from the driver and his client. It wouldn't be long before the police were on their trail.

"You're nuts."

"A little."

Trent handled the car like a NASCAR pro at the Indy 500 without a care in the world. It was apparent he was operating on full adrenaline. Marci was too, even though she hated to admit it. She was having fun. Adventure was what she always wanted. Except for the fact that her life really was at stake. That terrified her. When they finally made it out of DC, Marci sighed in relief.

Responding to a question she hadn't asked, Trent said, "We'll swap cars in Arlington. Ditch this one on the side of the road."

"Works for me."

About halfway home, sirens went off behind them. Trent glanced in his rearview mirror.

"Shit."

"Lose them."

Marci had recommended the unthinkable. They had no chance if caught. His eyes showed half confusion, half excitement. He floored it. The new Lincoln had some power, not as much as the cop's charger. At least Trent could drive. They merged onto a highway and blended in with the traffic. She swore they had lost them.

"You're unreal behind the wheel."

Trent's face lit up like he had never been complimented before.

"Don't flatter me until we're safe."

He made his way through the cars and shot off a left exit. Like that, they were headed west. The road opened before them. Marci exhaled.

"Not that I care, but where are we going?"

"No clue."

Marci should have been worried. Oddly, she was as relaxed as she had ever been. She trusted Trent, this stranger she just met, even after Pierce screwed her over. Any family of Lou's was a friend of hers. As the thought popped into her head, Trent's phone rang. He looked down.

"You might want to answer it," Marci said.

The phone rang a few more times. She grabbed Trent's cell. Extraordinary times called for extraordinary measures. Trent said nothing. He didn't seem to mind.

"Trent Rollins's phone. Who's speaking?"

"Ms. Rollins?"

"No. I'm Trent's friend. Marci."

"Hi, Marci. This is Lou's nurse, Sharon. We met the last time you visited Lou in the hospital."

"That's right. How is he?"

"That's why I called. Is Trent there?"

"It's your uncle's nurse."

Marci handed the phone to Trent. Her heart pounded. Something was wrong. It wasn't her place to demand an explanation from the nurse. Trent listened, his face contorting with emotion.

"I understand. I'll get back to you on next steps."

He quieted, then hung up. Marci's heart sank.

"What happened to Lou?"

Trent shook his head. Marci instinctively understood. Lou hadn't died of natural causes. They had gotten to him. It was all Marci's fault. She killed Lou. Sorry wasn't nearly enough.

"I don't know what to say."

"You know what to do."

"Expose those pieces of shit. He didn't deserve the hand he was dealt. All he wanted was for you to be the hero who told a truth he couldn't. No matter the consequences, everyone deserves to know what's among us."

"You can count on me."

Trent veered off onto a side road and headed onto the highway, going north.

"Do whatever it takes to redeem him."

He was right. She was ready. "Jersey bound?"

"Navigate away."

Trent turned up the music and sped down the highway. Marci pulled up *Among Us* on her phone and typed a new blog post. The world might not have her document in their hands, but they needed to know what she was up against. If she didn't make it, she wanted *Among Us* to be her legacy. It would live on.

About three hours later, they were almost at Marci's house. They were finally in the clear. No one had followed them. She had scanned every rest stop when they took a detour once to fill up the gas tank and again for a quick bathroom break. They would come for them. Just not right now.

"You're welcome to stay with me. I know that's strange since we just met, but I feel like I know you. Lou was so special to me. He was more than a neighbor or a friend. He was family. His family is my family, too."

"Thanks. I really appreciate it." Trent half smiled. "Normally, I'd decline, but given our predicament, two is better than one. They'll stop at nothing to hurt you. I'll stop at nothing to protect you."

Two is always better than one.

She had always been a one. Alone. The situation wasn't at all the way she dreamed of having a guy stay with her overnight. It was still the best outcome to a terrible situation. Even if only temporarily.

Stop at nothing to protect me.

No one had ever said anything like that to her before. Not even her ex-boyfriends. She knew why. He took an oath to protect and serve strangers. She was no different. It warmed her heart all the same. She could pretend, even if for the night, that someone, a handsome someone, cared for her.

She pressed the code on her front door. It swung it open.

Marci gasped.

CHAPTER THIRTY-FIVE

PIERCE AWOKE WITH A START. Turbulence. Only he had no recollection of boarding the ESA's private jet. He rubbed his eyes so he could see more clearly. Miles sat across from him in the plush leather chair. He was getting his shoes shined. The knowing smirk on his partner's face was unsettling to Pierce.

"That will be all," Miles said to the shoe-shiner, who scurried away.

"What's going on?"

"You've had quite the rest."

"Where are we going?" Pierce's voice was small and scratchy. He had to clear his throat a few times.

"To finish what you were too weak to do alone. You failed your assignment. This is your last chance."

Pierce's stomach swirled. The memories of the warehouse came back to him. He hadn't killed Marci. She had gotten the best of him because of it. He was ruining his stellar ESA reputation for a woman he barely knew. All because he believed she had more to offer the world alive than dead. He would have to prove that to Miles and the rest of the ESA before they took matters into their own hands.

"We'll get the document. Then we'll terminate Marci."

He hadn't meant it, about terminating Marci. He would work on a plan to convince her to come to their side to save her life. In the meantime, he had to persuade Miles he was on the ESA's side. The fire behind Miles's eyes said he wasn't at all satisfied. Miles brushed off his suit.

"I hope you mean that, Pierce. Your words haven't convinced me. Nor your cagey demeanor."

Pierce took a deep breath, swallowed hard, and adjusted his posture. He wrapped his mind around what Miles wanted from him. Pierce pulled memories from all the times he had to push forward through situations where he vehemently disagreed with the ESA's call to action. Miles shot Pierce a devious side smile. One that sent shivers straight through him.

"I assure you. I'm your man."

"I'm still not convinced. Although, I think I know precisely what will help to change your tune. Permanently. We don't have popcorn for this, but I think my short feature will keep you glued to your seat nonetheless."

Miles slid the tablet out of its leather case and placed it on the table facing Pierce. Miles hit play. The gray and white mini-mansion stood as it had for the past ten years: stunning, stoic, and silent in the night. Surrounding trees barely moved in the slight breeze. A seemingly peaceful night surrounding the house was eerie. The videographer's intent was nothing less than sinister. Nausea rose up in Pierce's throat. He watched and waited for what he dreaded but knew would come.

He held his turbulent emotions inside his heart. He told

himself that he was watching a movie, some fiction story, and not real life. His real life.

The man behind the hidden camera made his way to Pierce's front door. He didn't knock. He didn't need to break in either. It was the dead of night and whomever the ESA sent to Pierce's home was a professionally trained criminal.

Pierce caught sight of Miles smiling in his peripheral vision. *Bastard.*

The hitman passed a card in front of Pierce's front door. It unlocked automatically. The man was using an ESA-issued skeleton key of the highest technological power, not of this planet. He creaked the door open slowly. The house was dark and silent, as expected. The man barely made any sound as he strode through the first floor. He knew exactly where he was going. Systematically and heartbeat by heartbeat, Pierce raged against himself. He knew what was to come. He lied to his mind all the same.

Miles was silent as he looked as if he was watching and waiting for Pierce's reaction. No matter what Pierce watched on that video, he would remain calm, emotionless, and poker-faced. Miles would never see Pierce's anguish. Ever.

Inside, he was dying a slow death. All he could think to do was pray for mercy.

The man made his way up the winding staircase. When he reached the landing he paused, as if to let Pierce, whom he likely knew would be watching, digest what was about to happen. He took deliberate steps down the carpeted hallway, still silent. No need to alarm his victim.

The door opened slightly. The man peered in. There she was. Peacefully at rest in their king-sized bed. She looked like an angel. Pierce wasn't sure if he could watch any longer. He had no choice in the matter. Miles was analyzing his every reaction.

The man made his way to Lindsay's bedside towering over her. Although he didn't make a sound, Lindsay stirred. She opened her eyes. A look of terror in her expression shattered Pierce's heart. Worse yet was her face when the man, without audible reaction, gave her a lethal injection. Miles stopped the video.

"Next time you cross the ESA, the star of the show will be you."

Pure fury rose up in Pierce. It was unlike anything he had experienced before. He was ready to take the life of the person who had ruined his. It wasn't Marci.

"I'm ready now."

Miles grinned. "I knew the video would give you the final push you needed."

The captain came on over the loudspeaker. "We're headed for our final descent into New Jersey. Please make sure you are seated and your seatbelts are fastened."

Pierce held himself together, knowing it would all come to death blows sooner than he had imagined. His life as he knew it was over. No one was going to make it out alive.

CHAPTER THIRTY-SIX

PIERCE TOWERED over Marci and Trent as they stood in the doorway to her house. They aimed the extraterrestrial weapons at him that they had no business using. He looked as though he had grown an inch taller since she last saw him. He had puffed to a size broader at minimum. His face showed no emotion. He was cold, dangerous, and terrifying. His eyes looked dark as if they had changed colors. It wasn't his irises. Rage was growing within him.

"Drop them. You have no idea what you're doing. You'll kill us all."

"That's the plan," Marci said.

Three oversized special agents were suited up behind Pierce. Their broad shoulders touched, military-style. They were poised for immediate action. No emotional expressions lived on their faces. Only a laser-sharp focus that couldn't be shaken. They would kill her in the blink of an eye if they were instructed to or provoked in any way. They were itching for the signal to pounce, as they shot laser beams onto Marci and Trent's foreheads.

Trent elbowed Marci. She aimed a laser above the

middle agent's head and fired. A hole the size of a basketball seared through her wall. Pierce raised his hand. He turned to Marci.

"Do not even think about shooting that weapon. I just saved both of your lives. I don't think I can do it again. Their instinct is to kill. These agents will override me the next time. For the sake of your lives, drop those weapons."

Trent lowered his first. He knelt to the floor and placed the weapon on the ground.

"Drop it, Marci. He's serious."

Marci was shaking, tears streaming down her cheeks. This was her only chance. She was going to blow it. She promised Lou like he promised his family. Acting was the only option.

"I can't."

Pierce blocked the agents as they made their way toward them.

"You have no choice. You'll die before you can take another breath."

"Listen to the man, Marci. Please," Trent said.

Marci backed away from the door a few steps and bumped into Trent's rock-hard chest. A sense of relief washed over her. The terror of reality returned. For a split second, she considered pushing Trent out of the way and running as fast as her feet would take her far, far away from her home. She would be caught eventually. Trying to escape from the giant mess she had made was futile.

Lou was dead. Now Trent's life was in danger. All because she had to push a personal agenda that was way above her pay grade. She had no business getting involved in confidential government work, especially when it came to top secrets like intelligent life in the universe.

Trent traced his arms over hers from behind until his

hand was on the weapon. She released the tension in her arms and relinquished the gun to Trent. He placed it on the ground next to his.

"Done," Trent said.

"Give me all of them," Pierce said.

Trent slid the bag of Pierce's weapons across the floor in the agent's direction. Marci grunted. She pushed forward, right past Pierce into her home. Trent followed. Marci turned slowly to face Pierce.

"Level with me. What's all this about? People can't be dying over a fifty-year-old piece of paper."

Pierce laughed. "If I tell you, I'll have to kill you. Or worse."

"A fate worse than death? I'm willing to take that chance."

Pierce closed in on her. "That government document isn't just a fifty-year-old piece of paper. Humanity's existence depends on whether we retrieve it from you or not."

"I call bullshit." Marci's hands went to her hips.

"It's embedded with an invisible code that only the government can decipher. The letter Lou stole was the last piece of a puzzle we can't afford to misinterpret."

"Liar."

Pierce put his hands on Marci's shoulders. "As you can understand, the document in your possession is a critical component of national security. You must turn it over to us immediately."

Marci squirmed away from Pierce. "Too bad for you. I told you already. The document doesn't exist anymore. I destroyed it."

A flash of anger crossed Pierce's face. A look of resolve followed.

"We need to make it re-exist. It's plan B. You're not

going to like it."

"That's not possible."

"Everything is possible."

He gently nodded to one of his agents, the most robust of the trio. In a flash, he was securing Trent with zip ties. Trent struggled against them. It was no use to fight back. They would always win. Her job was to learn to how to play their game better than they did.

"I'm the one you want. Trent doesn't know anything."

"He is out of it. I can guarantee you that."

Trent wailed loudly. Marci turned to around. The agent pummeled Trent to the ground to subdue him. He shoved a needle in his arm. Trent went limp.

"That wasn't necessary."

"We can't afford any more mishaps. The Agency isn't kind when we screw up."

Sadness grew in his eyes. Marci paused. Something had changed the game. Pierce was all in now.

"And you're right, Ms. Simon. We only want you. Trent is collateral damage. Without that document, all we need to access is your mind," Pierce said with an edge of coldness.

A burst of anxiety shot through Marci. What were they going to do to her mind? The prospect terrified her more than any physical or emotional harm they could ever cause. Her mind was the strongest part of her. In it was the only truth she believed. What if they did something to change it forever and she would never be the same? She had no doubt they could do whatever they wanted.

"You can have me, my mind, whatever you need. Don't harm Trent."

"With all due respect, which I'd like to add, you didn't earn, we don't need your permission to do anything."

Pierce gave the agent who subdued Trent a look. He

scooped him up and carried him out of Marci's door. She spotted an oversized black van with tinted windows parked in front of her house. It hadn't been there when she arrived. Pierce tilted his head toward the remaining two agents, who rushed to his side in response. He took a step closer to Marci and whispered with a sinister tone.

"You've done enough damage."

"One last chance to hand over the document to us so no harm will come to you, or to Trent."

"What aren't you hearing? It's gone. Destroyed. No longer exists."

"Sadly, I can no longer be responsible for your fate. As you can imagine, the Agency doesn't know how to show mercy to those who betray them."

"The document you want never belonged to me. It was Lou's. Now he's gone. It belongs to no one now."

"It's not protected by copyright laws, Marci. It's not a novel. The government generated that letter and Lou stole it. The Agency is simply responding to his crime to retrieve their data. The moment I let you slip through the cracks in DC, the Agency responded again. Only this time, my wife, Lindsay, was the victim."

Marci opened her mouth to speak, then closed it. Her heart wanted to say she was so sorry for his loss. The right words didn't come. He was not a good man. That was clear. His wife didn't deserve to die for his wrongdoings, especially if he really had been trying to do a good deed to save Marci's life. Lindsay Austin's execution was all Marci's fault. Pierce blamed her for his loss. The anger behind his eyes said it all. He would never let her get away with that.

"I didn't ask for any of this. I don't want to be responsible for people's lives. It's too much of a burden for one person. It's much too much for me."

"Too late, Marci. You're committed to our cause for the long haul. The moment you took possession of a government document that didn't belong to you, one with critical information that could jeopardize the lives of humankind, you forfeited your ability to deflect responsibility."

"I still can't help you. Like I said, the original document has been destroyed. All that's left is the electronic version I already shared. There's nothing to retrieve. Nothing to turn over. It's gone."

Pierce walked over to the window and gazed outside. Safety in suburbia was a sick joke. Cedar Lane was full of secrets, lies, and betrayal. Innocent people died for nothing. Marci couldn't stop the agents from kidnapping her and doing whatever they wanted to her—making her disappear or worse. Assuming Lou's letter would be her ticket to getting her beliefs on the universe heard and understood had gotten her into this mess. Risks existed. She hadn't fully comprehended the weight of them all. In truth, she brushed them aside to push her own agenda. Lou and Lindsay were dead. Who was next?

She didn't have a choice. Pierce was right. If she wanted to have a chance to survive, to give Trent that same chance, she needed to do whatever it was the Agency wanted her to do.

She would acquiesce. Her life as she knew it would be over.

Steaming hot breath on her neck told her someone was behind her. She stiffened and then relaxed. Whatever they did to her would hurt less if she weren't so tense.

"That's too bad. I was hoping for a better outcome."

Pierce's words sliced through her before the needle stabbed her in the neck. Marci collapsed in peaceful surrender.

CHAPTER THIRTY-SEVEN

TWO-INCH-THICK GLASS SEPARATING PIERCE, Miles, and the other three agents from their subject was only a few feet in front of them. Pierce observed while the ESA's elite medics did their magic, swiftly attaching mini clear wireless electrodes head to foot on Marci's entire body. The synchrony of her mind and body would assist in pushing the buried images in her psyche to the forefront to be analyzed. Once Marci was prepped thoroughly, the ESA Analytics Program Director, Gerald Burns, addressed the handpicked team.

"We're about to begin. As a reminder, I'll be the one navigating the output strategically to find the answers we haven't been able to glean through research and observation thus far. More specifically, we're looking for the classified document. You are not here to simply observe the investigation and retrieval process, as some of you who have served on my analytical team know. I expect each of you to pay close attention to the hidden details shown here today. Your job is to communicate with me via the individually linked electronic pads embedded at your station. I'm relying on you to catch anything I may have missed so I may alter my direction to focus on items pertinent to this case."

Burns gestured toward a screen on the opposite side of the room.

"Your feedback will be shown and saved here, where we can analyze it later if the need arises. No talking. Are we ready?"

On cue, each team member gave Burns a silent thumbs-up. He flipped the switch to turn on the signal that communicated with the ultra-techno computer program only the ESA had access to use. The program came directly from extraterrestrial advancements. No person in Pierce's lifetime, no matter how genius, could create a device that could download, analyze, and interpret the human mind and experience.

Once the program began to output the data, the glass in front of them metamorphosed into a display where all of Marci's point-of-view memories, thoughts, and visualizations flashed before them in the form of eerily lifelike holograms as if the watcher lived behind Marci's eyes. Director Burns had the fascinating responsibility of sifting through her infinite images to find precisely what the ESA needed, not only the document but the key to who Marci was—her story.

With killer focus, Burns scrolled past seemingly infinite numbers of unimportant images of Marci's early childhood. Few notes were being taken, from what Pierce could tell. A faint glimmer of light caught Pierce's eye. He referenced it on his device, marking it for an urgent review, which was rarely overlooked. If he had learned anything in these scenarios, it was that if you were lucky enough to spot any sharp, illustrious, flickering images of light, it usually only meant one thing.

Burns glanced at Pierce. The director's eyes told him the data would be reviewed after the document was retrieved. Burns's brain appeared to work as fast as the alien intelligence-based computer, knowing precisely what to focus on and what to move beyond. Pierce wondered if Burns was part alien. It wouldn't have been surprising. Nothing had surprised Pierce since he joined the ESA ten years ago.

As expected, Burns narrowed the images down to the last month alone. From there, he focused on images specific to Marci's interactions with Lou Rollins. Finally, he found one with the document. He stilled the frame, zoomed in, and took a 3D scan. He printed an exact replica of the classified government document Lou stole over fifty years ago. Because it wasn't an electronic version but a clone, the hidden code should have appeared intact and easily decipherable. It would have been the document's doppelgänger and no different in any way than the original.

The seemingly impossible process was nothing new for Pierce. He had watched countless contents of human brains being downloaded, analyzed, and printed into physical forms for ESA use over the years. However, delving into someone's mind to retrieve a document that, once deciphered, would give humanity the answers to the universe was monumental.

Pierce pushed his seat away, about to stand up, when Burns rewound the memories in warp speed, stopping abruptly on a scene in what looked like a bedroom. He played it like a movie, with the grainy images in fast forward slowing to a high-definition stop. The small, short lump under the layers of covers told Pierce that Marci was only a child in this memory. Her twin bed butted up against the wall in her tiny room, with a window at the foot of the bed.

Through her half-open eye, Marci fixated on light coming toward her window. She quickly shifted into a sleep position, pulling the thin sheet over her head. When her eyes opened, the muted visual of two monochromatic figures appeared at the foot of her bedside. Through the sheet, they resembled the more common alien life forms. They were taller and didn't seem to have faces, which was another species entirely. Pierce was aware of at least a hundred different alien species that had been reported to visit Earth. Identifying them was a matter of scientific analysis, not photographic evidence.

A slight rustling at the bottom of the bed. As quickly as they arrived, the twin beings vanished. When their brilliant light retreated into the sky, Marci ripped off the covers. She hunched over and grabbed her right foot, examining the bottom. She rubbed the arch where a barely visible pinhole had formed, as if from a splinter.

Burns stopped the video.

"Thank you, agents. We have precisely what we need. Now, let's get to work."

CHAPTER THIRTY-EIGHT

COLD, gray concrete walls closed in on Marci. Her accommodations were more akin to a prison cell than a post-surgery hospital room. Groggy and in a drug-induced haze, the foot bandage was all that told her she had been operated on. A stiff mattress beneath her had no give whatsoever. She struggled to find comfort. Every time she moved, even ever so slightly, the shooting pain in the sole of her right foot nearly stopped her heart, electrocuting her with pain. Looking around the room, nothing indicated where she was or how she had gotten to the bed. She assumed it had everything to do with the ESA and Pierce Austin.

Nothing was in the room except her bed, a wheelchair and a small camera mounted in the far right corner. Her door had a small window. No way could she make it there on her bum foot. Unless she crawled. Her mouth was so dry it hurt. Dehydration was an understatement. She began to push herself up to a sitting position, hoping the camera would see her movement. A string tickled her neck. She reached for it and pulled it close to her. It was attached to a speaker and a button, exactly like they had in traditional hospital rooms. She pressed the button. Nothing happened. She pushed it again and spoke into it as loudly as she could muster.

"Anyone there? I need water."

No one responded immediately. She put her finger on the button to push it again. The door to her medical cell creaked open. Pierce walked into her room. She pulled the bed sheet up to her chin to cover her makeshift hospital gown. Marci was mortified that her enemy had seen her in such a vulnerable state. Then again, he had put her there in the first place. He handed her a liter bottle of water.

"You rang."

She wished she could refuse the water bottle. Refuse him altogether. She was more dehydrated than she had ever been in her life. Her throat felt like it was lined with sandpaper. Her tongue was like a razor blade. She needed liquid more than she needed her pride. Marci gulped down about a third of the fluid. She exhaled in relief.

"Where am I?"

Pierce raised his eyebrows. "You look like shit."

"Thanks. Do you plan to tell me what happened to my foot?"

"We cut it open. Like the document you tried to conceal. Your body was a guardian of classified information."

"I have a top-secret foot? You've got to be kidding me."

A laugh bubbled up in Marci's chest. She almost let out an uncontrollable giggle from hysterics. Anger quickly took its place.

"No kidding here."

"Now that your Agency finally has everything it wants, you can tell me the truth."

Pierce eyed her as if he was unsure of how to proceed

with the conversation.

"Do you remember your childhood, Marci?"

Like in a psychotherapy session, her doctor sitting across from her triggering a PTSD episode, a flash of memory attacked Marci like a lightning strike. They had visited her in the dead of night. Those inhuman creepers stalked her bedside, studying her in silence. Even at only five years old, she had felt their arrival in her bedroom. Their unfamiliar presence loomed over her night after night for what seemed like years. She pretended to be asleep, never opening her eyes all the way to see them in their entirety. They were there nonetheless. She was too afraid—or maybe too curious—to confirm who or what was standing there, watching her as she slept.

Marci shook it off.

"There's a lot about my life I don't remember. Like how I got here in the first place, and what you did to me after I arrived. Is Trent still alive?"

"He is."

"Can I see him?"

"Not yet."

"When?"

"I don't know."

"When can we get out of here?"

Massive anxiety flared inside of her. She couldn't simply walk out of there. Leaving wasn't on her terms. It was a prison. The surgery and the drugs all should have given her a reason to panic. As her wits came back to her, what she really wanted was control of her life again. Pierce looked down for the briefest of moments. What he was about to say wasn't going to be what Marci wanted to hear.

"That's not going to happen. The ESA does not intend to let you go. Ever."

CHAPTER THIRTY-NINE

THEY'LL NEVER LET me go. Pierce's words stabbed Marci in the chest. She could hardly breathe. She paid her dues. Followed the rules. Did what was expected of her. She never did anything against the law. Maybe a speeding ticket here or there. Nothing jail-worthy. Here she was in prison. For life. None of it made sense.

"They have their document. What else do they want? I have nothing left to offer. They can't keep me here against my will."

Marci sat up in bed, no longer worrying about what she looked like to Pierce or anyone else. They could keep her there forever if they wanted. She swung her legs over the side of the bed. No wires were attached to her.

"They want your DNA. It's exceptional."

Marci never had thought of her DNA at all. Let alone that it was exceptional. It's not as though she were a genius or a supermodel, or anyone extraordinary.

"They have it from my surgery. Big deal."

"It's not that simple."

"What are you talking about?"

"Unwelcome visitors came to see you while you were sleeping. You were only a child."

"How did you know about them?"

"During one visitation you were terrified. You hid under the covers, pretending to be asleep. When they left, you felt different."

"My foot."

"Yes. They did something to your foot."

Marci stared at the blank gray wall in front of her. She was trying to project the image from her mind so she could recreate that night and understand what happened to her all those years ago.

"I thought they put something in my foot. I felt it. I saw it that night. The next day the scar was gone. I told myself it was all a dream. I let it go. I was a kid. What did I know? They never came back. At least I don't remember it if they did."

"They didn't. But they've been keeping tabs on you from afar ever since."

"Did they install some tracking device inside of me?"

Marci grabbed her foot. She caressed her skin, frantically searching for a bump she had never seen before. Her foot throbbed in time. It was pissed at her for speaking ill of it.

"There's nothing in your foot."

Pierce walked over to the camera and clicked it off. He made his way to the door and turned the deadbolt. Marci sat upright. She was concerned he might hurt her. Pierce put his hands up in the air.

"I needed to make sure we didn't have any ears listening. Or eyes watching."

"What did they do to me?"

"They altered your DNA."

"That's ridiculous. There's nothing different about my DNA. I've had blood tests every single year. No one ever said anything."

"You were a sick child, Marci. You were diagnosed with a rare terminal cancer at only five years old. No cure existed. Your parents resolved themselves to the fact that you wouldn't survive. Instead of focusing on treatment, they let you live what little bit of life you had left being happy and ignorant to the truth."

"Where did you get this information?"

"You didn't have treatment because it would only have made you suffer without adding any benefit to your quality of life. Other than the occasional bout with exhaustion, you lived ignorantly with no evidence you were dying. It's exactly how your mom and dad wanted it to be."

Memories of spending months in bed as a child came storming back to her.

"There's no way you could have known all of this. Even I blocked it out."

"It gets more unbelievable."

"I'll brace myself."

"Shortly after those otherworldly beings visited you for the last time, you were cured."

Pierce was right. Marci recalled her later childhood years. Her experience was vastly different. She played outside more and was increasingly physically active over time. In high school, she graduated as a track star. She had always assumed it was because she was bored and wanted to get out of the house.

"Oh my God."

"Your doctors and nurses dubbed you Marci the Medical Miracle. Your parents fought for the news of your cancer disappearance to stay quiet. They didn't allow the truth to get out. They wanted a normal life for you.

"Everyone involved in your diagnosis and palliative care kept silent. The ones who threatened to expose the story for their own good were made legally quiet. Separation agreements and hefty severance payments always do the trick. In the end, the only people who knew what happened to you besides medical staff were your mom and dad."

"The government knows everything. Now they want me."

"They want your altered DNA."

"They have it from my surgery. They can release me now."

"It's not that simple. They don't want a sample. They want *all* of it."

"It's mine. They can't have it."

"You don't understand. You cannot deny the ESA. They'll ruin your life as quickly as they ruined mine, their loyal agent. You're a vessel to them. Nothing more."

"I'm done listening to this insanity. They have everything they've asked for...and more. I want to leave, and I want to leave now. Who do I need to speak with to make that happen?"

"You can't just leave, Marci. But you do have choices."

"The only thing I want is to leave this shithole, go home, take a hot shower, drink a giant glass of whiskey, and read a good romance. I'm done with sci-fi and horror. They're not fiction to me anymore."

"Stay here as a guinea pig. Your mind and body will be used for the scientific advancement of which you may never see the results. Your DNA may be used to cure diseases like cancer, or it may be used to create biological weapons. You'll never know."

"I'm never staying here. I don't care what they do with my DNA. That's on them. I just want to go home."

"Or trust me with your life. I'll do my best to have the ESA hire you to join our elite team. We'll partner with you, using your experiences and voluntary DNA donation to understand interplanetary relationships. We may be able to communicate with other species to find out why you were chosen for such technological advancement and what's in store for humankind's future. If you agree, I'll make a strong case to the ESA that your full cooperation will be worth much more than merely the use of your bodily fluids and tissue. But I need your one hundred percent buy-in. Not merely the appearance of it."

"I would never agree to either of those options."

"There are no other choices. If you fight me, I'll be forced to sedate you. I'll turn the camera back on and walk out of this room and your life forever. You'll be in the ESA's hands. I won't be able to help you ever again."

Marci wobbled over to Pierce. Her injured foot pulled behind her.

"You think you're helping me now? Look at me. I'm already your science experiment. Your prisoner. The only endings for me are leaving through that door alive or dead. That's your choice."

She dove for the bulge on Pierce's waistband, ripping the pistol out of its holster. He grabbed the syringe that looked like a pen sticking out of his shirt pocket instead of fighting her. He was too late. She pressed the barrel of the weapon into his fleshy temple.

"Stop, Marci."

"I may look small and weak, but I'm full of rage. I'm not afraid to pull this trigger."

Beads of sweat fell from Pierce's brow. "Don't do it."

"Drop the syringe. On the bed."

Pierce didn't hesitate and tossed it onto the mattress. With the gun pointed at his head, her eyes were fixated on his hands. Marci walked backward. Her hand searched for the small tube. When the plastic hit her fingertip, she snatched it up in her palm.

Pierce's attention shifted. He went for it. Marci held the syringe on her left side, the gun on her right. Only this time, she held it to her own head.

CHAPTER FORTY

PIERCE SLOWLY BACKED away from Marci with his hands up in the air. He hoped the ESA hadn't figured out what was going on.

"Don't hurt yourself. Please listen to me."

"I'm done with you telling me what to do."

"Once they find out this camera isn't working they'll be in here. We don't have long."

She tapped the gun to her head. "That's why you're going to help me escape. Or you lose everything."

If Marci died, he *would* lose everything. "You don't want to kill yourself. Think about what you're doing."

"I'd rather die than become the ESA's next lab rat. Worse yet, your protégé. You've done nothing but lie to the world for your own personal gain. Sacrificing human lives for technology. You're all murderers."

"I understand you're upset, but please don't hurt yourself."

He panicked with the outcome she was threatening. The ESA wouldn't only kill him if this went bad. They would torture him first. This case was his ticket to the top.

Not only of the ESA hierarchy. If he was given credit for finding the link between human disease and an extraterrestrial cure, even if the government wouldn't let the truth out right away, the opportunities were endless. Without Lindsay, the ESA and his career were all he had left.

"You haven't seen my version of upset."

"You're reacting out of anger. You don't know the whole story. Let me help you understand everything."

"I understand everything that needs to be understood. The only way I'm no use to the ESA is if I'm dead. Otherwise, they'll always be at my back. I can't live like that."

Tears streamed down Marci's clenched face.

"I can handle the ESA. You're worth much more to the world than you think. The ESA can take a back seat this time if needed."

"I know my worth. I'm a human being whose life has been sabotaged for good—or for evil, I'll never know. My life has never been my own. It never will be. It's time to take it all back. Even if through death."

"You don't know what you're saying. You can save all of us if we go about this the right way. Let me help you."

"If you were a reasonable person, I'd believe you. You're not. You're a liar."

"Your life depends on you believing me right now."

"They'll never let me out of here. Will they?"

Pierce shook his head. He was her only hope. By the look on her face, she knew it.

"Not without me."

"Then you'll need to take me out."

"They won't let me do that."

"They will if they think you're taking me somewhere for testing. Then you'll let me go. If you try anything funny, I'll pull the trigger."

"I'll do whatever you want."

"Get that wheelchair. Bring it to me. I need your ID."

Pierce followed her directions. He pushed the chair until she grabbed it. Marci put her hand up to catch the security badge. Pierce tossed it in the air like a Nerf football.

"Now take off all of your clothes."

"Excuse me?"

"You heard me. Strip down."

"You're going to get us both killed."

"Kick your clothes over to me. Turn around."

He followed her directions exactly.

"Now what?" A gown landed on his shoulder.

"Put it on."

When Pierce looked up, Marci was already dressed in his clothes. Her hair was tied in a knot and folded under to look like his short-cropped cut. She held the wheelchair out to him.

"This will never work."

"Get in."

Pierce sat down. His heart raced at the thought of a foiled plan. Marci was messing with the most powerful government agency in the world. An agency that managed to keep extraterrestrials a total secret for decades. They were capable of destruction beyond Marci's wildest imagination. She was playing with a volcano and had no idea. A trait that would have made her crazy enough to be his partner. Marci threw a blanket on top of Pierce.

"Cover yourself. Keep your head down. Out of view."

Out of the corner of his eye, Pierce spotted how confidently she slipped his mirrored glasses on as if this were the role she had been waiting her whole life to play. While shorter than him, Marci's stature wasn't off base. She could have passed for Pierce on video. Especially if no one was looking too closely. He assumed that was what she was banking on.

Marci headed to the camera and pressed the button to turn it on. She quickly turned around to face the doorway with Pierce. After pushing the gun up against Pierce, out of sight, she rolled him into the hallway.

"Which way out?"

Pierce tilted his head and pointed to the left. Marci shoved the barrel of the gun deeper into him as if to remind him of what she might do if he didn't cooperate.

If Marci got caught, her death would be a catastrophe the world could not afford.

CHAPTER FORTY-ONE

MARCI'S HAND squeezed Pierce's shoulder. She whispered in his ear through gritted teeth.

"I told you to keep your head down. Where's Trent?"

Pierce tilted his head to the right.

"Where are the testing rooms?"

He nodded in the same direction.

"Cough when we arrive."

She rolled Pierce down the hallway with purpose. The ESA's maximum security, technologically-driven laboratory prison didn't have a need for physical security. Cameras and sensors told the ESA all they needed to know. So long as Marci could fly under the radar for long enough to get an escape plan together in her head, she may be able to pull it off.

Frigid cement floors boomed under Marci's steps. It was dark and gray, not unlike an abandoned facility. The ESA was working from behind the scenes. They trusted Pierce, but one false move on Marci's part and they would be all over her. Losing the most valuable asset the ESA had ever discovered wouldn't bode well for Pierce.

Pierce wanted to pick his head up to analyze his surroundings. It was too risky. He had to use his memory to find Trent. He had no idea how they were going to add a third person to the escape plan. He wasn't about to argue with Marci now. All he could do was defend her life when, not if, the time came for a confrontation with the ESA.

About halfway down the hallway, Pierce coughed at the only door in their sights. Marci pulled up short to the cell. She lifted on her tiptoes to look into the window.

"Trent's gone."

"He's not there?"

"Where would they have taken him?"

Sheer panic in Marci's voice was palpable. Pierce had no idea. He was supposed to be in his cell until they handled Marci. Trent would have been terminated next. It was possible they ended him already. Telling Marci that would only enrage her. He told her the only thing that would deter her from looking for him any further.

"If he's not in his cell, then he's in the lab," Pierce lied.

Marci's shoulders fell. Realization filled her desperate expression. It was now or never, and she had to leave Trent behind. Marci pushed Pierce in the direction of the lab.

"We're going."

She was insane. "You can't do this. They'll figure us out. Then it will all be over. No escape. No mercy."

Marci didn't respond. She smoothly and forcefully pushed Pierce's wheelchair down the hallway until she reached the end. The double doors were locked. If she activated his ID, the doors would open. Everyone would be alerted to her arrival.

"We can't go this way. They'll know."

"Where can we go?"

Pierce tilted his head to the left. A small hallway that seemed to lead to nowhere appeared.

"Turn here. It's a back entrance for medical personnel. If you scan my card, no alarms will sound."

Marci paused for a moment. She hightailed it down the hallway and out of camera sight. When she reached the end, a badge scanner with a blinking red light appeared. When she flashed Pierce's ID in front of it, it changed to green and silently unlocked the door. She opened it with her left hand, pushing Pierce through with both hands. Marci would stand out in his uniform, and he needed her to be discreet. His job was to protect her now, no matter the outcome. He pointed to a set of lockers that were never locked.

"Stop here. Grab a lab coat. You'll be better camouflaged."

He watched her as she opened one of the doors, grabbed a long lab coat, and threw it on. She shoved his glasses and hat in the pocket of his ESA agent jacket. Someone's glasses were left on the top shelf. She put them on. He hoped her vision still worked. They both needed to get out of there alive.

"Where to now?"

A series of smaller passageways came into view. He could fool her and take her to a dead end, or he could take her to the lab, where she wanted to go. He needed her trust, primarily if they survived her crazy plan. He pointed to the right.

"The back door to the lab. You'll be able to see everything before you go inside. If you choose to."

He hoped she didn't.

When they pulled up to the door, the large flat screen outside the door was on, as usual. The intent was to let medical personnel know if they were in surgery and at what stage, for both training purposes and surgical procedure assistance. No need for an agent to use this entrance. They had other ways to get into the lab. The threat of being discovered was minimal.

Marci and Pierce watched as a team of medical professionals hovered over an operating the table. Much like Marci, various probes and wires protruded from the area, attached to nearby machines for data to be analyzed. Pierce looked up. The devices weren't connected. It wasn't possible. To delve into someone's body and mind to the extent the ESA did for their experiments, a series of machines kept the person alive while they monitored their progress to ensure none of the injections gave them life-threatening reactions or killed them.

"What are they doing?"

"I'm not sure." Pierce knew precisely what they were about to do. It wasn't surgery. It was an ESA autopsy.

When several of the doctors stepped away, Marci gasped. Trent was nowhere to be found. An alien corpse was sprawled out on the medical examining table. An incision opened its torso wide.

"We shouldn't be here."

Marci's head snapped left to right. "I can't leave without Trent."

"You don't have a choice. If you want to live, we need to get out of here right now."

CHAPTER FORTY-TWO

MARCI GRIPPED the handlebars of the wheelchair until she was white-knuckled. *An alien autopsy.* She nearly passed out at the sight of it. What had they done with Trent? What would happen to her? Their predicament was all her fault after all. Lou and Trent were only trying to help. Lou was dead. Trent was missing. Or dead.

"I said...we need to go."

Marci snapped out of her reverie. She spun the wheel-chair around and headed to the main hallway. She had to pass Trent's room one more time. They would, hopefully, all head out together somehow. When she got to the end of the medical hallway, footsteps distracted her.

"Shit."

"Someone's coming," Pierce said.

Marci pulled the wheelchair over to the side. Still aiming the gun at Pierce, she peeked around the corner to the main hallway. A group of three officers approached. Her heart rattled against her ribcage.

"Now what?"

Pierce gestured toward a closed metal door. "We can hide in that supply room."

Marci spun the heavy metal chair around once again. She rushed to the small door fifteen feet away. The men's footsteps were getting closer. She didn't want to panic. Working off adrenaline and instinct, she wasn't thinking about her actions.

She thrust the stainless door open. Plenty of room for both of their bodies inside. No way would the wheelchair fit through the narrow opening.

"Get up. Get into the closet."

He followed her orders quickly. She pressed the gun against Pierce's torso until he was entirely inside the room wedged between a shelf full of medical supplies and a giant vacuum, which she was sure wasn't meant to clean the floors.

Marci carefully wheeled the chair a few feet away from the door. She ran to join him in the small room. She quietly pulled the door closed until it latched shut. She turned the little lock on the inside. The room was almost all dark except for the light bleeding in from the hallway. Their troubled breathing was the only sound. They both seemed to notice it and slowed to a near silent stop. Marci had the gun trained on Pierce. He didn't even try to move an inch.

Her eyes adjusted. She turned to examine Pierce. He looked like he had aged years since she first met him. A vulnerable sadness lived behind his expression. She sensed his cold demeanor was all a facade, a casualty of working for the ESA, one she couldn't imagine. Marci hadn't been a vibrant person. Most of her life she considered herself quite dull. Yet the letter Lou entrusted her with had added a spark of excitement to her world. She was full of purpose. More alive than she ever had been. Now that she had lived that way, she would never be able to live unconsciously again.

The present moment was everything to Marci. Every sight, sound, and emotion became a beating heart inside her. She moved in a way she never had before. Drive and passion ruled her from the inside out. Exposing the truth was Marci's calling in life. She would never going back to the silent, rule-following, fake Marci from academia ever again.

Deliberate footsteps grew louder as they drew closer to them.

Pierce mouthed to Marci.

"They're coming."

He put his finger up to his lips. She squeezed her eyes shut like she did as a small child when she didn't want to see the truth. In her head, if she couldn't see them, they couldn't see her. This was more a coping mechanism than a reality. It comforted her. In that moment of danger, comfort was all she needed. No way to escape.

As if Pierce could read her mind, he ignored the gun shoved in his gut and put his arm around Marci's shoulder. He gently pulled her close. She didn't resist. She released the gun and fell into him. If they were found out and Pierce was right, she believed he would protect her for no reason other than she was truly valuable to the ESA. The ESA was all he had since Lindsay had been murdered, which was also her fault. If they opened that door, it might very well be her last moments alive and of her own free will. Her free will was to accept the human condition, the one she so desperately wanted to preserve and embrace with another human being.

He held her tightly as if she were all he had left. No words were exchanged. The energy between them told her that she was safe. Even if it was all a ruse, she held onto that belief for survival. The plastic soles pounded the concrete hallway floor. They were getting closer.

"What the hell is this," the first agent to speak said. "These people don't do their jobs anymore."

Their footsteps landed right outside their door until they slowed to a stop.

"We don't pay them enough," the second agent said.

Pierce carefully covered Marci's mouth as if reminding her that any noise was deadly. She exhaled. For the first time in her life, peace engulfed her soul. Even though the protector was her enemy.

Shadows of their shoes broke the streaming light on the floor.

"We're not on wheelchair duty, fellas," the third agent said. "Admin will take care of it."

CHAPTER FORTY-THREE

MARCI HELD HER BREATH. Termination didn't mean the same thing to the ESA as it did to the rest of the world. She wondered who wouldn't wake up tomorrow because of her desire to escape. A rush of guilt swarmed her until she remembered whom she was dealing with. They killed people for a living. Was Pierce the same way? Her eyes darted up to see him. He looked down at her; peace fell over his face. Why wasn't she afraid? She went with it and relaxed her shoulders.

The agents' heels grew quieter as they made their way down the hall toward the operating room. Pierce released his hand from Marci's mouth and loosened his grip on her waist. She pulled away from him.

No sound of the agents anymore. They were gone. The dynamic between Marci and Pierce had shifted. The energy they shared was no longer adversarial. Forcing it to be so would prove unnatural. Marci considered all Pierce had said to her. She had no choice but to trust him now. She was vulnerable once again. This time she didn't care.

"Can you get me out of here alive?"

Pierce's eyes were kinder somehow. He spoke softly as if she was more to him than an experiment. She was his friend.

"I'll do my best."

She checked the shelves behind them and found stacks of scrubs.

"You can't run around in a hospital gown. Take your uniform back. I'll put these on."

They turned around with their backs to each other and changed into their respective uniforms. She tossed the lab coat on the floor. By the time someone found out what they had done, she would be long gone. Marci unlocked the closet door. She cracked it open an inch.

"What's the fastest way out of here?"

"We can go back the way we came, toward the medical area. We already know those agents went that way. One of them will be summoned to retrieve the wheelchair. Let's go back toward the main hallway. There's a door to the stairs that I have access to unlock. We can get out through the basement."

"I'm in."

"Follow me."

Pierce grabbed Marci's hand and nodded to the right. What choice did she have? She allowed Pierce to pull her down the hallway at a pace that was unnatural. Time was running out. It wouldn't be long before the ESA's cameras were examined and they realized she wasn't in her room and wasn't scheduled for any examinations or interrogations. Pierce had gone missing as well. They had minutes, maybe seconds to escape.

She spotted the door marked as an exit. Pierce practically dragged her to it. He reached for his ID and fell short.

"We need to scan my badge."

"Don't you have it?" Marci swore she had given it to him back when they were changing.

"No. Where is it?"

Marci frantically patted herself down. All the worst-case scenarios flashed through her mind. This was all her fault.

"I can't find it. Maybe I gave it to you?"

"You've got to be kidding me."

"I'll go back. Maybe I dropped it in the closet."

"We don't have time," Pierce said.

"We don't have a choice."

Marci turned to go back. Footsteps bellowed again. Pierce reacted before she had a chance to figure out what was going on. He grabbed her shoulder and pulled her into a slight alcove near the stairs. She spotted an agent patrolling the hallway, checking on prisoners and protocol. He would soon find out Marci wasn't there. Pierce pushed Marci to the back wall, only a few feet from him. He reached for her gun. She hesitated before obliging. He was the only hope she had. He waited behind the wall like a cop on the attack, with his gun close and aimed at the ceiling. Once the agent passed him, he grabbed the back of his neck and put the gun to his head.

"Breathe too loud and I'll kill you."

The agent struggled. Within seconds, Pierce had his arm around his neck and silenced him with a chokehold. The agent dropped to his knees. Pierce kicked the slumped body out of sight. He grabbed his badge and gun. He gave Marci back his gun. They were both armed. She was surprised but grateful she had trusted her gut. No matter his motivation, he really was on her side, even if just for now.

"Let's get out of here."

Pierce headed for the stairs. Marci followed close

behind as he swiped the badge until the door to the stairwell opened. They ran down several flights until they reached ground level, which was the ESA's basement. When they opened the door, it was a large area. A parking garage without any cars. Instead, containers lined the walls of the room.

"What's in those? Aliens?"

"We don't keep them here."

They were harboring aliens. Pierce had confirmed it. She wasn't sure if she was shocked or impressed. She followed Pierce to one of the containers. He swiped his card in front. It opened right up on cue. He entered the metal tube. Plenty of space to spare for a few more people. It almost looked like an elevator without an apparent shaft. He reached his hand out. She hesitated for a beat before she got in.

Pierce scanned his badge again. The cylinder door slid shut. He pressed a button before entering a code. An iridescent green LED light came on. Marci's stomach dropped as the tube lifted away from the surface.

CHAPTER FORTY-FOUR

WITHOUT LOOKING DOWN, Marci instinctively reached for Pierce's hand. He was her only hope. He wrapped his fingers around hers and held on tight, pulling her close to his side. Marci was confused. She was blind as to what would come. Pierce's guidance was all she had at that moment. She had surrendered to him. She trusted him. Pierce's heart warmed in response.

Together, they silently stepped onto the open field, high above the buildings from where they had been on the run moments ago. The rush from the helicopters left them helpless. Wind gusts temporarily deafened and blinded them. Escape had meant capture, once again. No running away now. Unless they wanted to dive off a cliff to their death.

Trent Rollins stood large and robust before them. His arms crossed in contemplation. He donned an ESA agent's uniform, fully equipped with weapons and ammunition. A dozen men dressed in military garb formed an army behind him.

"You made it," Trent said.

Marci whispered to Pierce. "What's happening?"

Pierce looked genuinely confused. "I have no idea."

Trent grabbed Marci, handcuffing her. The gun dropped out of her hands.

"Why are you doing this to me?"

Trent didn't answer. Miles followed suit with Pierce.

"Is this necessary?" Pierce asked.

"It sure is, partner."

Miles pushed Pierce forward until they reached the helicopter. Pierce hopped inside the aircraft, and Marci got in after him, with Miles and Trent following close behind. The helicopter buzzed. It lifted off the ground into the air above DC.

"Pierce," Miles said. "You're pathetic, you know that?" He shook his head. "Now, Marci, I can understand. She's a second-rate teacher from New Jersey. But you? A government-trained secret agent with access to the universe's infinite capability sides with our most important subject."

"What's he doing here?" Pierce stared down Trent. "Shouldn't he be locked up in a cell somewhere?"

Trent was cold-faced. "Funny how roles can reverse so quickly. How an arrogant prick like you can be so blind as to the actual truth."

Miles patted Pierce's thigh in an otherwise affectionate gesture.

"I knew you were shit the minute you turned on me in DC. The ESA is much smarter than you think. You were high risk from the very beginning. You produced for us. You did what needed to be done, no matter what. We gave you some bottom-of-the-barrel work over the years, too, but you never faltered. We still watched your every move. You were a little too flashy and a little too arrogant for your own good. The ESA is a clandestine organization, yet you acted as if you were an Academy Award-winning actor working the red carpet. You took liberties. You put our great nation—and the world—at high risk for exposure and invasion."

"Why didn't you just eliminate me?" Pierce shrugged.

"Oh, silly Pierce. You still don't understand how this all fits together, do you? We needed you for our master plan. Marci isn't just any captive, but you know that already, don't you? I'll hand that much to you. You did your research on her. You know her worth. Even if the ESA plans to use her for selfish means. Damned emotional being inside of you, the one you haven't fully suppressed, can't come to grips with the fact that her life means something important to humanity and our interplanetary pact. And you're not wrong." He laughed. "See? I do give credit where credit is due."

"You didn't answer my question," Pierce said.

Trent leaned forward. "About me?"

Marci turned to Trent. "What's going on? Why are you with them? I thought something had happened to you. I wasn't going to leave without you. I was so worried. Your uncle..."

"Oh for God's sake, enough about my uncle," Trent said. "He was a righteous prick who thought he knew what was best for the world. Imagine that? One old man who had all the answers to the universe."

"He was your family." Marci's pained expression broke what was left of Pierce's heart.

"Bullshit. He came into my life when he needed my help. I was suspicious about his intentions years ago. I knew he was a threat to the country's security, so I did a little digging. I found mention of the ESA in one of his old papers. Nothing telling. It aroused my curiosity. I did what any loving countryman would do, I told my story to the FBI, which led to the CIA. Shortly afterward, lo and behold, the

ESA came knocking on my door. I held nothing back. They listened to me tell them everything I knew, as well as my suspicions."

"How could you do that to him? He loved you." Marci looked away, not waiting for Trent's answer.

"Easily. My so-called *family* was an ex-general, anti-government traitor who had access to top-secret information —snippets, but enough to potentially bury the ESA if they got into the wrong hands."

"You're a bastard." Marci shook her head. "He was a good man."

"We knew you would get sucked into Lou's insanity. One government document with the secrets to the entire universe? Come on." Miles chuckled. "We're not living in a blockbuster movie."

"Lou's letter was the last one we needed to solve the puzzle. Stop the charade," Pierce said.

"You academic types think you're so clever. Just because you have a Ph.D. in some useless subject you think you know it all," Miles said. "You think you know what we do and how to do it, and what's right." His face twisted into a devilish grin. "You have no idea."

"He's lying," Pierce said to Marci.

"And you, Special Agent Austin. I'm so disappointed in you. I truly believed we could mold you into the conformist agent we needed. Heartless. Fierce. Deadly. Instead, you turned into a moral-seeking family man with an affinity for young professors who believed in the possibilities of the universe." He rolled his eyes. "The truth is the truth no matter what you believe. And the truth is, you were duped."

"Excuse me?" Pierce said.

"That document was planted. In Lou's safe and his

mind. It never existed. None of them did. Why would the government put such details in writing, ever?"

"Are you losing your mind, Miles?" Pierce asked.

"Planted," Trent said.

"For what purpose?" Pierce asked.

"None of this makes sense," Marci said.

"When we found Trent, he was very forthcoming and willing to do just about anything to help us out. We knew General Rollins had access to top-secret information that was no lie. Instead of simply eliminating him, we decided to make a game out of it. Marci conveniently lived across the street. We began to dig and had reason to believe she had been of high interest to extraterrestrial beings. We needed proof to understand her role. When we learned, we knew we had to push them together on a mission somehow."

"You set all of this up?" Marci asked Trent.

He raised his eyebrows in semi-agreement. Miles chimed in.

"Not all of it," Miles said.

"There were things we truly didn't know about you and your past," Trent said.

"We needed to look inside your mind," Miles said.

"It only told part of the story. The part that was unable to be proven if investigated. Uncle Lou had the physical pieces to put the story together without the document. We chose to make it easier for him. We needed someone who would make it his or her personal mission to challenge us."

When the helicopter landed safely on top of the White House, it quieted. Marci straightened. Pierce shuddered. This was par for the course, protocol in situations as dire as theirs. The President of the United States was the silent head of the ESA. If it had gotten to the point of his involvement, they were in too deep. Powerless in more ways than

Pierce could imagine. This is where it all started. This is where it all would end.

"Shall we?" Miles asked.

Trent pulled Marci onto the rooftop. Pierce hopped down. They made their way to a heavy metal door on the backside of the White House. It opened.

CHAPTER FORTY-FIVE

PIERCE WEAVED through a series of secret hallways with Marci by his side. Trent and Miles led the way. White House staffers were oblivious to the underground tunnels' existence. They were designated for authorized ESA use alone.

Once they reached the basement, the hallway opened into an entryway. It faced a large room bordered by tinted glass. Marci stood next to Pierce, with Trent and Miles sandwiching them in the middle.

The glass silently receded into the wall, disappearing before them. It exposed a giant American flag hanging on the far wall behind a marble table with three chairs. Six gigantic security guards lined the doorway. They split in the middle to let the party of four into the room.

They took a few steps into the room and stopped. Marci took an extra step. She corrected herself and got back in line with the others. The director of the ESA, Joseph Beckford entered the room. He sat down in the middle seat.

Marci and Pierce began the long walk toward their two

chairs facing the table. Empty seats on either side of the ESA director awaited Miles and Trent. Pierce had been on the other side of the table presiding over cases many times. He wasn't in charge now. He hated that.

Pierce sat down first. Marci followed suit.

"What now?"

"We wait for the ESA director to call upon us."

"You say it like it's a dinner reservation. My fate is in these psychopaths' hands."

"Remember, they need you."

Marci stared at the floor. Giving in was inevitable. Giving up wasn't an option. Pierce rolled his shoulders back. He held himself a little taller. Maybe his false confidence would persuade Marci to be strong like she always had been up until that point. He had been honest with her. They did need her. They would save her. He was another story.

Pierce had lived to support the Agency. His life's work was to serve humankind, even if in an unconventional way. They had lied to him. Used him. Manipulated him. Pierce hadn't deserved it. He had been loyal to the ESA. They had turned their backs on him in the end.

As Miles passed by Pierce on his way to the front of the room, he whispered in his ear.

"One more thing, my old friend. Getting rid of Lindsay wasn't only necessary. It was my divine pleasure."

Pierce lost all sense of control and logic. He lunged at Miles. Pierce headbutted his partner with intense force. Miles was more a concrete wall than a person. Pierce tottered on his feet, swaying side to side. His head pounded. Stars formed before his eyes. Nausea grew. He was going to pass out. He didn't have to wait long. The pinprick of a needle pinched his skin. Warm fluid slowly entered his bloodstream. His body turned to jelly.

Pierce's vision faded to gray before it disappeared.

CHAPTER FORTY-SIX

MARCI STIFFENED. Frozen in place. The shocking scene played out before her in the depths of the White House. She had lived her life in a bubble knowing far less than she ever imagined. She was fighting the all-powerful establishment for a truth she believed in so deeply. Losing at a record pace.

One of the burly guards was dragging Pierce's limp body out of the room. His legs and arms slid across the floor like a rag doll. The ESA director didn't flinch. He observed the incident as if the cleaning crew had arrived to mop up a puddle before they could get started with their agenda. No emotion lived behind his eyes. No compassion in the way he watched his staff handle another human being. Pierce was an object to be dealt with. Nothing more.

Marci wanted to scream aloud for them to stop. Not to hurt Pierce or else. She didn't. There was no *else*. Nothing she could do. She had no power, be it physical or otherwise. One of their own, an agent who had dedicated his life to their work and had followed their rules to a fault, meant nothing to them. Pierce was the epitome of loyalty. It hadn't mattered. He was an object to be controlled. Like everyone else.

Marci had no recourse. If she attempted to lash out or escape, she would discover the same fate. Her insides were jumping up and down on a trampoline. She remained poised in her chair. Once the doors closed behind Pierce, and the guard left, the commotion subsided. Everyone settled in their seats. Marci was left alone to face the all-powerful ESA. The defendant in the trial of her life.

"Welcome to the White House, Ms. Simon. I'm Joseph Beckford, the Director of the Extraterrestrial Security Agency. Special Agents Rollins and Gordon will oversee this case. I'm here to monitor as well as interject as needed. Any questions before we get started?"

Marci had a thousand questions. Why had they kidnapped her? What really happened to Lou? Why was Trent a bastard? The last thing she wanted was to appear combative or angry, even though she was both. She had a right to know certain things. All things. After everything that everyone had been through, she wanted answers immediately.

Marci swallowed hard. Her mouth was drier than sandpaper.

"Why am I here?"

"Why do you think you're here?" Trent asked.

His tone sent shivers through her soul. The use of reverse psychology wasn't surprising. His ease in appearing cunning and manipulative was what unsettled her to the core. He was not the same man who had saved her life. No longer the empathic state trooper who told her two was better than one. Not in this case, apparently. No human emotions were present in that room. Trent's demeanor was the real persona of an underground agent that no civilian ever wanted to encounter.

Now that Marci had, she wondered if she would ever be free again.

She thought about her answer. It wasn't what the ESA wanted. They wanted her perception of his response. She recalled everything that had happened up until the present moment, all the accusations and glimpses into an ESA agent's life. She told him what he wanted to hear. An ego stroke would get her farther than an attack.

"My actions were a threat to our freedom."

Trent raised his eyebrows. "You're catching on."

Miles sat back in his chair. "Deep and accurate. But not entirely true."

She was confused. All the while Pierce and Miles had been acting like her access to information and desire to reveal the truth was the issue. If the public knew about the evidence the ESA had been withholding from them for decades, their trust of the government would be gone, chaos and outrage would take over, and the security of our entire planet would be threatened.

"What did I miss?"

Miles smirked. He regained his naturally cold demeanor.

"Your actions were futile. They never did much of anything but waste the ESA's precious time and money by chasing you up and down the east coast."

"Threatening me initiated the chase. I didn't run from you by choice. I was hunted."

"Pursued is a better word, professor," Trent said.

"I gave the ESA everything I had. They never let up, coming after me ruthlessly. They threatened me repeatedly. It wasn't enough. Lou died anyway."

Lou and Lindsay had been caught in the crossfire of her life adventure. They hadn't deserved the hand they were dealt. Marci's desire to expose the government had killed innocent people. Her selfishness appalled her. Who did she think she was?

It all came down to one thing: their deaths were her fault. Now it would be her mission to avenge their deaths.

"There's a long-standing history with Uncle Lou that predates the birth of most of the souls in this room."

The realization of the truth hit Marci hard. "You're admitting your men killed him?"

"Your interpretation is your own," Miles said.

"He didn't die of natural causes like the hospital said, did he?"

Trent shrugged. "Uncle Lou was in possession of a document that did no harm being locked in a safe all those years. The older he got, the less of a liability it was for him to have it. The document was common knowledge at the ESA. Lou's hope for the truth to be shared with the world was no secret either. The only problem for him is that he wasn't strong enough to take that on. You're a different story."

Marci's heart was full. Her eyes filled with tears. She held them in. No time to cry. Time to act. Sharing the truth had been her only goal. The public had a right to come to their own conclusions, not the ones fed by the ESA, POTUS, or otherwise. Strength to do whatever needed to be done came from Lou's confidence in her. Entrusting her with something so valuable had made all the difference.

She thrust her chest out. "Damn right I am."

Miles leaned forward. "Fun fact, you weren't the first person General Rollins gave access to that document."

Marci's heart sank. She caught Trent's gaze. He was

looking at her with cold eyes. The recent events that had seemed disjointed and chaotic began to fit together like puzzle pieces.

"The ESA needed me for more than the document."

"Uncle Lou got the ball rolling. Then the ESA systematically lured you here. It wasn't an easy path. The fire inside of you is stronger than we ever anticipated."

"I don't understand what you want with me. The document is in your possession. You've looked into my mind. You've searched my home. I have nothing more to give you. You captured me. Why haven't you killed me yet?"

"What we do in the Office of the President of the United States is maintain order in a world full of rogue maniacs, bullies, and murderers. Civilians can't possibly understand how extensive our job is to keep everyone in line and safe."

"Your job isn't to keep everyone in line. It's to ensure freedom. Lies aren't freedom. They're deceit. Truth is freedom."

"The bad ones are already here. I think you know that. We must keep global peace. Peace comes with ignorance. Truth creates mayhem. When there's mayhem, people die."

"Our truth is deadly. A fact you'll soon learn," Miles said.

"At your hands it is."

Trent looked Marci straight in the eyes like an opponent. He wore a contradictory smile of sincerity. He was fierce. So was she. His devious eyes shimmered as if the sentiment behind them wasn't disgust. It was admiration.

"We never cared as much about the evidence as we did about you. You became the key to it all. We didn't want to let you go."

CHAPTER FORTY-SEVEN

MARCI SHRUGGED. "You got me. I'm already your prisoner. From the looks of it, you never will let me go."

"True. We could exert our power and force you to do what we want. If you're going to serve the purpose our nation needs, your heart must be in it completely," Trent said.

"I'm not in anything with you people."

"Not yet."

"Not ever."

"You're special, Marci. Unique and extraordinary. The ESA respects those qualities immensely," Miles said.

"Respect isn't caging me like an animal. The ESA takes whatever and whoever they want and use it to their advantage. I'm a human being just like you, Trent. Flesh and blood. I have a heart and soul. None of which is up for debate. Or governmental use."

Beckford pushed away from his chair. He headed toward the exit without a word. Guards followed close behind. He left the room. The door slammed. Silence filled every space around her.

Contradiction and confusion loomed. Beads of sweat tickled Marci's forehead. That was it. She had she gone too far. It was over.

Once the ESA director left the room, Trent's demeanor shifted. An aggressive agent no longer sat before her. Gentle kindness washed over him. He looked more like the man she had met in Virginia. She wanted to trust him. Wished she could be vulnerable with him. But she had been burned before. Trusting anyone wasn't an option.

"We've all said enough. Let us give you an opportunity to experience everything for yourself."

For her safety and the safety of where they were headed, *so she was told*, Trent and Miles flanked Marci. They met up with Pierce, now coherent and cooperative. They walked together like they were on the green mile. Still their prisoner, she got into an elevator in a darkened, almost invisible hallway in the depths of the White House. More nooks, crannies, and mysteries existed in the president's home than she ever imagined. It was haunted in so many ways. Part of her never wanted to leave the place until she explored every inch of it.

When the steel doors closed, Miles waved his forefinger over a black scan box. A red light flashed. They took off like a rocket. The elevator shot downward as if in a free fall. No floors were labeled in digital lights. No buttons to press. Fingerprints alone operated the elevator. Only the universe knew where she was headed.

Straight to hell.

"I trusted you, Trent."

"You still can."

"I risked my life for you."

"I risked mine for you. I would do it again."

"Don't do me any favors."

"You're doing me one. I used you because of my belief in the ESA's program. Once you know the whole truth, you will, too."

"Don't bet on it."

Trent had betrayed her along with Pierce. They had set out on a childish game of cat and mouse to serve her on a silver platter to the ESA like something an animal dragged in. Nothing they did or said would change her mind. Her truth was her mission.

The government that should have brought her freedom was controlling her and everyone else in the world. That was the real truth. The public had no idea.

"They played me, too," Pierce said with an embarrassed tone.

It gave her a sick sense of comfort to know she wasn't the only one duped. They had betrayed one of their own agents. Pierce had to have trust issues ten times over on her.

"I appreciate you trying to make me feel better. That wasn't fair."

"I was in on it all along," Miles said proudly.

The doors cranked open. They disappeared inside of the elevator shaft like pocket doors. Pitch-dark blackness consumed Marci. Trent patted her shoulder in a kind gesture before falling into line with Miles. She shuddered. Her shoulders tightened. She didn't want to move but had no choice.

"Ladies first," Miles said.

"You'll be all right, Marci. I promise," Trent said.

"I'm here," Pierce said.

"Let's get this over with," Marci said.

Pierce linked arms with Marci. "This won't be easy. I'm right next to you."

Her shoulders fell. Out of all the deceit she had experienced, Pierce had been right in the end. Pierce's words had comforted her, even if they came at a price. They walked in the darkness. He led the way for Marci. It was as if he had been there millions of times before. He likely had. Marci took several deep breaths. She tried to prepare herself for what she was about to experience. She had been waiting for this opportunity her entire life. No preparation was worthy enough for a life-changing encounter. Everything about her, who she was and what she believed in, would be forever altered.

Blackness blinded Marci. She allowed her mind to embrace the darkness before her. Going with the flow had never been easy for Marci. She didn't have a choice now, so she made the best of it.

No natural light existed. As they got farther into the space, dim laser lights lined the creases between the wall and the floor. Everything around her was made of what looked like stainless steel. The vast area was clean, sleek, and cold. Nothing like she had ever seen before. She wasn't sure what purpose it served. She would soon find out.

When they arrived, she found a line of circles stamped on the floor. Before she had a chance to ask what they were, Pierce chimed in.

"Do what we do. That's all. Simple."

Pierce stood on one and lit up with a blue light underneath him. The rest of the ESA agents stepped on their circles. Marci was the only one left. One ring remained next to Pierce. She took a few steps forward and landed on her circle. All the rings lit up in yellow in unison.

Before Marci took her next breath, she was drowning.

A stream of hot water rushed down on her like a waterfall emanating from above. She choked on the water until she realized what was happening. Her own private shower had appeared, without tile, glass doors, or a curtain. Fully clothed, no less. No soap involved. After the water permeated every inch of her, it disappeared through tiny holes in the floor below her feet. Seconds later, a rush of air filled the same stream. It was drying her from her hair to her feet. When the wind tunnel evaporated, a pleasant-smelling perfumed mist engulfed her. Full body deodorant, she assumed.

Marci breathed in as much oxygen as she could get before suffocating once again.

A clear tube shot up from the floor. It encapsulated her completely. Claustrophobia set in. Apparently no one at the ESA got the memo about her anxiety disorder. More likely, they didn't care. The tunnel initially made of hard plastic metamorphosed into a thin cellophane wrap. It closed in on her, sticking to every inch of her skin from her shoes to the base of her skull. An oval-shaped helmet formed at her chin. It bumped out from the cellophane and created a perfectly fitting body suit. Oxygen flowed through freely to her lungs. From where, she didn't know.

A voice spoke to her from inside her helmet.

"You can speak when you're ready. We'll all hear you. A two-way microphone system is embedded in the suit," Pierce said.

"Thanks." Marci was afraid to say anything more. Everyone, including the bad guys, was listening.

It was as if Pierce had read her mind. "No need to be afraid. This is the safest place on the planet. Follow our lead. You'll see everything you need to see."

Miles led them down the stainless-steel corridor until they reached what looked like a dead end. He scanned his palm in front of it. The wall split in half and opened, disappearing into the building. They walked through a series of glass doors until they reached an archway labeled RESEARCH LABORATORY. As soon as Miles got within a few inches of the door, it opened on its own.

Marci stepped into the vast space. Only a transparent wall separated her from the quiet yet buzzing energy of activity on the other side. At first blush, it looked like any other lab—unremarkable. Scientists wearing long white coats concentrated with intensity as they peered through microscopes. They mixed solutions in glass jars. Marci didn't know if they were intent on saving the world or destroying it. She was confident she was about to find out.

"Take a close look, Marci. It's your exorbitant tax dollars hard at work right here," Miles said.

Marci had no idea why the government would have some top-secret lab hidden miles under the earth unless their efforts would have been deemed taboo—or dangerous. Her courage shot to the surface. She tilted her head back, her chin pointing toward the sky.

"What are they working on?"

"Your DNA," Trent said.

CHAPTER FORTY-EIGHT

HER DNA. They were working on her DNA. The possibilities of what that meant terrified her at a primal level. All she could imagine were millions of cloned Marcis covering the planet. A scientific experiment gone terribly wrong. It was something out of a seventies science fiction novel. She had no desire to play the heroine.

"Soon you'll know why all of us risked our lives for you to be here," Trent said.

Marci rolled her eyes. "You did me no favors."

"No, but you did one for us," Trent said.

They followed the glass around a bend until they reached an oversized metal door.

"We're going in. Feel free to observe and ask any questions you want. Just don't touch anything unless you are given express permission. Your suit will protect you from the elements, but it will interfere with certain research experiments."

Marci nodded. She wanted to get on with it. All this time had been wasted. She needed to know the truth. For once, faith wasn't enough. This time, she had to see all they were promising with her own eyes to believe it.

The door whooshed open. They entered the lab in single file like grade school. Miles led the pack. Trent followed close behind, then Marci, and Pierce behind her. Slow and easy breaths reminded her she was at peace. Safe. They would protect her. She hoped.

Scientists went about their work. They ignored Marci and the agents. Tours must have been a regular part of their workday. Although she wasn't sure for who.

"Don't worry," Pierce said. "If you talk, only we will hear it. The scientists aren't tuned into our frequency. To them, we're silent observers."

"Got it," Marci said.

They walked past a series of unattended microscopes. Miles stopped in front of one of them. He waved Marci over.

"Step right up, professor. What you're about to see is going to blow your mind," Miles said.

Pierce nudged her. Marci cautiously walked over to the station.

Miles gestured to the eye of the microscope.

Marci pressed her eye to the viewfinder. She had no idea what she was looking at. How could she? She was an English professor, not a scientist. She had long forgotten about grade school experiments. The liquid moving around didn't blow her mind.

"It doesn't look like anything," she said.

"This is what civilians call life," Miles said.

A bunch of bubbles came into view, which she assumed were cells. They were very active, moving in the petri dish below the scope. The cells were alive. It was the coolest thing she had ever seen. They seemed to be simultaneously changing and multiplying at warp speed. Her mind was expanding. The fuse was lit.

"What is it?"

"We call it our lab rat," Miles said. "You'd call it Stage 4 cancer."

Marci drew in a deep breath. She covered her mouth. Her high regard for the killer before her disgusted her. She wished she could take her admiration back. It didn't deserve one ounce of anyone's attention.

"Ew," was all Marci could muster.

"Those larger distorted bubbles are the bad cancer cells, while the smaller perfectly round bubbles are the good, healthy cells. The distorted looking cells are taking over and growing, yet the perfectly round cells are stagnant. Move away from the scope for a second and watch what happens."

Miles summoned a technician over. Two dishes of cells that they were experimenting on sat on the counter. One tube of liquid was labeled with a C, and the other was marked with an X. The technician took a syringe. He extracted some of the cancer. After dropping it into the dish, he slid it under the microscope.

"The C is traditional chemotherapy for this aggressive cancer." The technician picked up a new syringe and proceeded to extract a measured amount of the chemotherapy from the C-labeled tube. He added it to the dish and slide it back under the microscope.

"Now look again," he said.

Marci peered down the lens. The newly introduced liquid methodically killed the distorted cells. It also rapidly killed the round cells. The round cells were all but gone. Half of the distorted cells were left. They were no longer growing, but disappearing at a slower rate, until they stopped. The remaining distorted cells floated around the dish. While they weren't multiplying, they were still surviving.

Marci pulled away from the microscope. Her stomach clenched. The best scientists in the world had spent their lives and billions upon billions of dollars in funds raised to fight a disease. Curing was a joke. The result was half-assed. It was beyond depressing.

"That's it?" Marci asked.

Miles winked. "Not so fast. Our coveted XNA enters the scene. Each droplet will match itself to the cells' natural DNA so it can fill in the mutated spaces to make the good cells whole again."

The lab technician extracted fluid from the vile labeled X this time. He repeated the process. Marci immediately went to the microscope to look. Exactly like Miles had explained, the XNA wasted no time getting to work. The round cells grew larger and stronger. The distorted cells minimized to nothing. Then they disappeared. Within seconds, all that was left was a dish full of healthy cells that appeared to be thriving. They moved faster than the distorted cells had before. Multiplied until they could no longer fit in the dish, they almost burst out, overflowing. They had more than adapted to their environment.

Marci pulled away from the microscope. She took a few steps back from the laboratory's station. She had experienced more in her life than most people. Miracles. Aliens. Now breakthrough scientific advancement. It was an unprecedented first. Not only for her. For the world.

Mind almost blown.

"Was that the cure for cancer in action?"

Miles smirked. "A synthetic version of the organic formula."

"Where's that?"

"I'm looking at her."

"That's not possible."

Marci wasn't sure if she was able to grasp what she had learned from Miles. She shook her head in confusion. Pierce put a hand on her shoulder.

"It's the truth. You're the only human being whose DNA has been merged with XNA and survived. Your body absorbed the XNA implanted in you when you were a sick child. It not only cured you. It melded with your cells and organically manifested the cancer cure."

"How can you know this?"

"Give me your arm," Miles said.

Pierce nodded. "Do it, so you can know for sure."

Marci should have been thankful that he asked instead of just jabbing her like he had done in the past. Miles took a nearby new syringe, unwrapped it from its paper casing. He pressed it up against a fleshy part of her bicep. He extracted a tiny bit of blood before grabbing an undisturbed dish of cells.

"Watch this."

Miles dropped her blood into the dish. He shoved them under the microscope.

She looked once again. Only this time it was mind boggling to her. As if in a flash, the cancer cells were entirely gone. The healthy cells restored to a full count, and then some. No time had seemed to pass. It was instantaneous. She pulled away from the microscope one last time.

Boom.

"Oh my God," Marci said.

"We didn't understand any of it at first. We knew you had extraterrestrial knowledge and power hidden within you, but we weren't sure what exactly. You seemed to know things, to believe things wholeheartedly that only someone who's been in the presence of otherworldly beings would have known. The letter was the key. It opened the door for us, but until we delved into your mind and experienced all that happened in your life, we didn't know you were unknowingly the original XNA experiment. We've been trying to replicate that formula for fifty years, ever since humans have been abducted and returned, we've been experimenting with their DNA. About ten years ago, we discovered the XNA. Unfortunately, the human already died. Apparently any human that was given the XNA died. Except you."

"You've had the cure for cancer in a lab and you haven't released it to the world?"

"We want to get it right," Miles said.

"People are dying every day from this horrible disease. It looks pretty right to me."

"That's the potential, sure. It looks like our scientists have mastered it, but we haven't been able to save everyone. You, however, have helped us with that."

"Me? I haven't done anything."

"Not of your free will. When you were under our care and observation, we took the liberty of extracting several vials of your blood to test. And, as we suspected, your blood cures all. With one manipulation, it has the opposite effect."

"I'm living a horror novel."

"It's for the greater good," Trent said.

"It is. If you cure people with it. That's not what you're going to do. It would put too many people out of business. Cancer is big business. Death is population control. What will you really use my blood for?"

Miles's sly smile gave Marci chills.

"Trent's right. All of this really is for the greater good."

She bristled. "I'll be the judge of that. It's my blood after all."

"Take a look for yourself. Then you can decide," Pierce said.

"Let's go then. What haven't I seen yet?"

"Most of it," Miles said.

They all turned and walked out of the proper lab and into what looked like a science experiment gone wrong. Marci stepped foot into the adjoining room. She held her breath. Doctors and nurses of all stripes worked on bodies on gurneys. None of them moved. None of them were hooked up to any machinery whatsoever. All different kinds of procedures were being done, yet there was no blood.

They weren't dead.

They weren't human.

CHAPTER FORTY-NINE

PIERCE HAD FINALLY GIVEN Marci what she wanted. Proof aliens did, in fact, exist. More than that, they were here already. Precisely as she had always suspected. Right there on the gurneys in front of her. It was just the beginning for Marci. Pierce prayed she would find the strength to handle everything she had seen and learned in such a short time frame. Marci's eyes bulged like an innocent child's in amazement and terror.

"Is this for real?"

"It's the tip of the iceberg," Trent said.

"There's more?"

"Can you handle more?"

"Hope so. You don't have much of a choice. POTUS orders. Last thing you want to do is piss that man off. No. No," Miles said.

Trent chimed in. "I know this a lot to take in. It's important for you to see everything so you'll know where you want your life to go when the time comes."

"Unlike the common mentality of the ESA, none of this is about me. Never was. Never will be."

Pierce could see that Marci understood innately what everything was all about. She would do the right thing when the time came.

"Let's go on to the next room," Pierce said.

"Now here's where the lab work goes to the next level. We merged extraterrestrial and human DNA right here. As a result, we may, in fact, be able to create a new race of super-humans."

"Why are you messing with human DNA?"

"It's flawed, Ms. Simon. Cancer is one of its flaws, but it has many others. I'm sure you've heard of them. They're called disease. Not only physical but mental, too."

"Stop the cameras from rolling on this bad science fiction movie."

"Bad. Good. It's all relative. The world might be a better place once we eliminate all the psychopaths. We don't need another serial killer strolling around town. Am I right, or am I right?"

Marci gave Miles a look of death.

"Then you'd have to be eliminated. Please let me be the one to pull the trigger."

"That's not the point. This is about preserving humankind," Pierce said.

Marci turned to Miles. "Please tell me how any of this could be happening under everyone's noses?"

"Let's move on to our final destination," Miles said.

They all followed Miles into the last room on the tour. The one that would shock and disturb Marci more than the others. The place where the puzzle pieces came together perfectly. The double wooden doors opened to what looked like a boardroom. It was set up like a movie theater.

"We're watching a movie now?"

"This is the last reveal. I promise," Pierce said.

Once everyone was seated in the room, Miles flipped a switch. The entire place went dark. The wall in front of them transformed into what appeared to be a high-definition display. Except it wasn't a movie screen at all. It was still the wall, only now it was made of glass. On the other side of the translucent display were all different forms of alien beings at work. Extraterrestrial beings were watching and analyzing human beings in pods. Aware they were being viewed, they seemed to revel in it.

"What's going on? I can't be seeing what I'm seeing."

Pierce grabbed her hand. This truth would hit her hard. Miles got up in front of the room to speak. He straightened his suit.

"This is our reality, Marci. Humans are no longer in charge of our great planet. About fifty years ago, your neighbor, Trent's uncle, retired Army General Lou Rollins was privy to top-secret information about the existence of aliens. Their existence was only the beginning. When they landed here, they learned of our vast population, resources, and our ability to procreate. They discovered our intelligence, as well as our ability to destroy ourselves. Some of them wanted to play nice and help us. While others wanted to destroy us and take over. To save our planet and humankind, we made a pact with extraterrestrial life. We would give them what they wanted in exchange for the latest technologies, both medical and otherwise. They could take some specimens for experimentation. We admittedly had to sacrifice some lives. In exchange, we would have access to advance our species far beyond our wildest imagination. And stay alive, the most important bargaining chip."

Marci's jaw fell slightly open. "Am I dreaming?"

Miles turned to look at them. "We never expected this outcome. We thought our pact would enforce a fair and equal trade. But as is true in most negotiations, one side loses more than the other. We were the side that lost. We didn't just lose human lives. We lost our freedom. Once they realized their power over us, they made Earth their second home. So long as we allowed them to do as they pleased, they would keep us alive and let us live here."

"Let us?"

Miles walked closer to her. "As you have witnessed, they don't only exist here, they thrive. They've been here, among us, all along. As long as we follow their rules and let them do whatever they want for as long as they want, we will get the gift of life on this planet."

Marci wore an expression of horror. "This can't be real."

"It is. Now you understand why we don't want humankind to know," Pierce said.

"It would threaten all of our lives," Trent said.

"It's not an option. But you do have one. A decision that will affect not only your life, but the lives of all of us."

"Why don't you just manipulate me to do what you want like you have in the past? Oh, because that's what you're already doing."

"We don't want to make you do anything," Trent said.

"We want you to choose with your own free will," Pierce said.

"If there's a choice to be made, I choose death. Living like this is hell on earth. I'm certain there's a peaceful after-life waiting for me."

Miles put his hands up. "We can't make you do anything. Sure, we can drug you and take your DNA. We can treat you like a captive. You would just die. Either from misery or your own free will. As you've said, you don't want to be here, so what good would you be to us dead? We'd rather you come to our side of your own free will. Not because we want you to, but because you would be protecting humans from the truth, which is the greatest gift you could offer."

"If I don't?"

"You'll be letting down the world," Trent said.

"I'm pretty sure you've already done that," Marci said.

Pierce turned to her. "The ESA can let you go. They'll take as much of your blood as they can. Erase your memory. But those ETs will always be watching you. You'll never truly be free. You just won't know it."

"Again, just kill me."

"Not one of your options," Miles said.

"Then I'll kill myself," Marci said.

"They won't let that happen either," Pierce said.

"I'm a prisoner for my entire life, one way or the other."

"We can let you live a quiet human existence. It will be a mundane life where you'll never truly fulfill your potential." Miles paused, seemingly for effect. "But isn't that the most pitiful hell on earth you can ever imagine?"

Marci leaned in to listen with intent. Pierce sat silently next to her. Support was all he could give right now. He couldn't make her do anything or change the facts of their lives.

"Or?"

Miles smiled wide. "Join the ESA as one of our top agents. We'll train you like our best. You'll be required to participate in some experiments, but you won't be a prisoner or a lab rat. You'll be used to serve your country. The only caveat is you can never tell anyone the truth you've learned today. Or you'll be terminated and erased from the minds of those you love as if you never existed."

"I understand."

Pierce honestly wasn't sure what she was going to do. He was at peace knowing she had all she needed to make her decision. Life on the run and in obvious danger was over. Marci was so much more than she appeared to be on the outside. He hoped she would find the path to her truth, no matter the obstacles ahead.

"We're almost ready to continue on with the next phase."

"I hope you'll join us," Trent said.

"I'll do what's right."

"I believe in you, Marci. Whatever you decide, I'll support you," Pierce said.

Marci's face fell. She seemed to finally believe his words, after all their difficulties and life-threatening situations.

"I know you do, and you will. It means the world to me. Unfortunately, I can't make everyone happy. I'm going to let a lot of people down, but I need to follow my heart."

Pierce's heart fell. The world would lose her if she didn't join the ESA. He didn't want to sway her, but he was afraid of her potential going to waste. He had to let go of it. It wasn't his battle to fight anymore.

"I appreciate your honesty. Following your heart is all I ever wanted."

Pierce put his arm on her back. He led her to the decontamination room. The private elevator would transport them to the Oval Office. Soon enough, the world would either have the benefit of Marci's value or not. He had no say in the matter either way. He had done damage. He had also made strides. Now it was all up to Marci. He watched as she straightened her shoulders, more confident than he had ever seen her.

The President of the United States welcomed only Marci into the Oval Office. The giant door shut with a thump.

CHAPTER FIFTY

EVEN WITH MARCI'S sunglasses on, the daylight nearly blinded her. The sun was so bright. It lit up the whole Jersey Shore. Her phone buzzed. It was a text from her mom wishing her luck. She needed it more than ever. Marci waited patiently as they announced her to the high-energy crowd. She thought she was prepared, but now her emotions overwhelmed her. She drew in a deep breath. She was up.

The president of Jersey Shore University took his position at the podium.

"Our commencement speaker needs no introduction. You know her as our very own Dr. Marci Simon. An English professor at Jersey Shore University, opening minds to the unknown since she stepped foot on campus. She has not only shared her knowledge with us but her friendship. You also know her as the blogger, ME Simone, who made headlines after using her curiosity and drive to teach us about bravery, strength, and passion through her public exploration of the unknown. She's known for questioning the unquestionable and opening the minds and hearts of millions with her voice. Today, we have the true honor of hearing her words of wisdom, not as a faculty member, but as a community leader, public figure, and friend as she turns her life's work into researching her first love, the vast cosmos. Only the universe could take her away from us, so please join me in welcoming the honorary Dr. Simon to our graduation ceremony."

The crowd cheered and clapped for Marci. Euphoria filled her heart. A sense of gratitude for the moment and her life took hold. Her love for the students and faculty of Jersey Shore University, no matter their history, was paramount.

Marci stepped up to the podium. She took it all in. The hundreds of kids wearing caps and gowns just like hers. The positive energy radiated, and her captive audience silenced to hear what she had to say. She spoke, not from a piece of paper, but from her heart.

"I'm beyond grateful for the warm introduction and for my time at Jersey Shore University. It's an honor and a privilege for me to be here with you today, and I promise to use that time wisely. I'm not going to preach to you about how to be a good person in this world, because I believe you already are good people. I'm also not going to give you advice on how to be successful, because I think you already are successful. I'm not going to share the secrets to happiness. As I stand here and look at all your faces, I can say with certainty that you know all about happiness.

"What I will stand up here and do is remind you of something you already know, but you probably need to hear at this critical point in your life. I'll leave it to one piece of advice, because there are so, so many things I could tell you.

You can easily remember one thing. It's more important than knowing anything else. So here's my one piece of advice from the universe to keep close to your heart as you go out into the world as the good, prosperous, and happy people you already are: the truth is the truth whether you believe it or not.

Now that you have my secret to the universe, may you go forth with this knowledge and live the glorious life that was meant to be all yours. Congratulations, graduates!"

The graduates rose to a standing ovation. Marci bowed in gratitude. She discreetly walked off the stage. She had held the spotlight for long enough. Now it was their time to shine. Besides, she was running late.

As soon as Marci was out of view, she ducked behind the stage. She ripped off her gown and cap, tossing them into a nearby garbage can. Faster than she had ever run, she bolted for a blacked-out SUV parked on the corner across from the university. The door opened before she could reach for the handle. A strong arm grabbed her. She leapt into the truck.

"Well done," Pierce said.

Marci strapped the seatbelt over her navy suit. She shook her hair out. Inadvertently, she caught a glimpse of herself in the mirror. The drab nude lipstick did her no justice. She pulled a ruby red gloss out of her pocket. Swiping it on, she barely looked in the mirror while she applied it.

"It worked out. That's all I asked for," Marci said.

Miles was in the driver's seat. Trent was his passenger. They sped off onto the interstate.

"Ready for your first assignment, Agent Simon?" Pierce asked.

Marci vowed to keep the promise in her heart to reveal

the truth one day, somehow. Until then, she looked back one last time to watch her beloved Jersey Shore disappearing behind her.

"I was born ready, partner."

THE END

ALSO BY KRISTINA RIENZI

ABOUT THE AUTHOR

Kristina Rienzi is a Jersey Shore-based new adult thriller author, certified professional coach, and the former president of Sisters in Crime-Central Jersey. An INFJ who dreams beyond big, Kristina encourages others (and herself) to embrace the unknown through her stories. When she's not writing or drinking wine, Kristina is spoiling her baby girl (and two fur-babies), dissecting true  crime stories, singing (and dancing) to Yacht Rock Radio, or rooting for the WVU Mountaineers. She believes in all things paranormal, a closet full of designer bags, weekly manicures, the Law of Attraction, aliens, angels, and the value of a graduate degree in psychology. Her debut audiobook, *Among Us* was featured on Audible's ACX University and is an Audible Editors Select pick.

Visit her online at
KristinaRienzi.com

facebook.com/KristinaRienzi

twitter.com/kristinarienzi

instagram.com/kristinarienzi

amazon.com/author/kristinarienzi

ACKNOWLEDGMENTS

First and foremost, I want to thank my family and friends for their understanding while writing *Among Us*. Countless times since I started this book back in 2016, I retreated to my writing cave instead of making memories. Specifically to Tom and Dad...your love and support has meant everything to me.

I also want to acknowledge my brilliant editor, John Adamus (a.k.a. *The Writer Next Door*), for his patience, dedication, and coaching. I never would have been able to pull this story off without you. Your insight has propelled me to new levels as a writer. My passion for the writing craft has been set on fire. I'm forever grateful.

I owe more than a chocolate bouquet of gratitude to my assistant, Kate Tilton. You come to the rescue every single time and you never let me get off course. I'm so impressed by your work ethic and your giant heart. You inspire me. Thank you for everything, but mostly for being YOU! This book was a long time coming. I'm finally publishing it because of you.

Finally, all of my writerly love goes to the writer and reader community.

There's nothing better than having a writer tribe to call your own. Sisters in Crime Central Jersey, thank you for allowing me to be your president for the second year in a row. It's an honor and a privilege to be a part of such an amazing organization. I'm so grateful to have you on my side.

Readers, especially my Rienzi Rebels, your excitement for my stories is what keeps me dreaming up new characters and adventures. Thank you for your support all these years. I write my books for you.

www.ingramcontent.com/pod-product-compliance
Lightning Source LLC
Chambersburg PA
CBHW021003120726
47905CB00009B/2839

* 9 7 8 0 9 9 6 9 7 2 1 6 1 *